PERSEVERANCE: A REFUGEE'S STORY

SAHEB EBRAHIMI

authorHOUSE®

AuthorHouse™ UK
1663 Liberty Drive
Bloomington, IN 47403 USA
www.authorhouse.co.uk
Phone: UK TFN: 0800 0148641 (Toll Free inside the UK)
        UK Local: (02) 0369 56322 (+44 20 3695 6322 from outside the UK)

Published by AuthorHouse 08/16/2022

ISBN: 978-1-7283-7459-8 (sc)
ISBN: 978-1-7283-7458-1 (e)

To my parents

ACKNOWLEDGMENT

The writing of PERSEVERANCE: A REFUGEE'S STORY would not have been possible without the assistance and advice of family and friends, including Eric Butler and Susan Clayton, Shân Wikeley, Stephen Evans, Brian Profitt, and Ray & Kate Morris. But I must especially acknowledge the loving support of my wife, Faezeh. Her faith and long-suffering through the birth pangs of this novel gave me strength to push through, as it was a very painful and personal story to tell.

Refugees are neither seen nor heard, but they are everywhere. They are witnesses to the most awful things that people can do to each other, and they become storytellers simply by existing. Refugees embody misery and suffering, and they force us to confront terrible chaos and evil.

ARTHUR C. HELTON

TRAVEL AT DUSK

Gripped by fear as the stinking lorry
Tossed around in darkness.
Surrounded by boxes, crates, and plastic sacks
Grapes, melons, and aubergines, indifferent to my miseries
Suffocated by the smell of rotting fruit
Not knowing where they are taking me was excruciating.
Where am I heading to?
My poor parents, how can they stand it?
Gawked at by the night.
Time seemed still, as if it were the end,
But I had to persevere, summoning up courage for the battle.
A matter of life and death it was—
My last chance to survive.
Awoken with a jolt against a box of cherries.
It became morning eventually. The rosy outlook of dawn,
But the thought of a possible arrest by the border guards
Was frightfully discouraging.
I wondered what lay ahead of me.
I knew that only time would tell.

CHAPTER 1

"Hop in now. Hurry up," the driver said, with a gruff voice. "Hide yourself behind the boxes."

He then gave me a blanket to cover myself. I felt helpless and scared, but I had no other choice than to obey everything he instructed me to do. He had promised my friend he would take me, and he had demanded a large amount of money.

It was dark. No one was in the street. It was nearly eleven when I left Armin's house. Armin was an old colleague of mine and the only person I could trust. He agreed to let me stay a couple of days with him until we could find a smuggler to get me out of the country.

The driver was a short, fat, middle-aged man with a black beard and a big moustache. He was wearing blue jeans and a black jacket. He seemed a reticent person, uttering only a few words.

Before we set off, I asked him where we were heading. He didn't reply.

"Please! Where are you taking me?" I repeated.

"A safe place," he barked with an edge of fury. I was scared. The thought of arrest by the plain-clothes police was giving me the jitters. I felt so troubled that I was not able to concentrate. I was thinking of my family. What would happen to them if the plain-clothes or security officers were to find the list or the things I left at the house church?

My parents are elderly. My father recently had open heart surgery. To treat his heart, doctors had his chest cut open. So my father needed special care to recover. Any stresses and tensions could put his recovery at risk. Doctors advised my family to be more cautious after the surgery, since there was a risk of chest wound infection or heart attack.

The driver threw a small plastic bag into the lorry through the rear window containing four plastic bottles of Damavand mineral water, a small red apple, a loaf of Barbari, Persian classic bread, and 100 grams of Mihan white cheese. I hadn't eaten anything for two days due to too much stress, so I devoured everything hungrily.

It was two-thirty in the morning. Time crawled slowly for me. The foul-smelling lorry jostled us around in darkness. We had a bumpy journey because the road was very rough. The rotten fruit and other items, which were suffocating to me, had been put there intentionally to distract attention if any of the police who might appear on the road searched the lorry. It was humiliating to find myself in such lowly and desperate circumstances.

I closed my eyes and struggled to sleep. A few hours passed. Suddenly, I woke up with a jolt. Losing my balance, I was hurled against the boxes. I was badly hurt by a sharp piece of wood from a broken box that punctured my back. Fortunately, it didn't hurt my spine. Then I returned to my hiding place and covered myself with the blanket. I closed my eyes and tried to sleep. I woke up again. I couldn't go back to sleep because of the bumpy road.

It was growing light. I could see this through the tiny holes I had made in the blanket in order to see the outside.

CHAPTER 2

"Police! It's the police! Plain clothes police! Everyone leave! Run!" cried out Mehran, in panicked terror. I went to the window to see what was going on. I could see plain clothes police jumping down from the wall into the yard. They were seven or eight, maybe more. It was then every man for himself. Panic gripped all of us. We had just one shared instinct—run. We fled down the narrow path at the back of the villa that led to the other neighbouring villas, and then to a wider path. My heart was beating wildly. I felt I was about to collapse. Yet some force was encouraging me to continue running. I ran through the hedges that separated the houses. The hedges consisted of shrubs and small trees which had thorns and prickles. Once I was in a taxi, I found out that I was badly injured, especially my hands.

The villa belonged to a member of a house church. We were a group of new Christians, men and women, who regularly gathered for worship in private homes. Every session we came together at a different place to avoid suspicion. There were usually nine of us. It was Mehran's turn to care for us. He gave out the Bibles to the members and was responsible for keeping an eye on the entrance door.

Suddenly, on the run, I realised that I had left my briefcase at the house church! I couldn't risk my life going back for it. Unfortunately, it contained my ID and a couple of books.

No doubt they will find out who I was and surely come to find me, I thought. The first thing I did was to remove my sim card to avoid being tracked by the plain-clothes police.

*   *   *

The driver gave me a quick pat on the knee to wake me up. We were somewhere near a steep and rocky cliff. Down the hill, I could see a village in the distance. It was a little cold there, but the landscape was stunning—peaceful, relaxing, and quiet. The sun was rising. I realised I must have slept for hours. The driver passed me a glass of tea and some biscuits. He then told me to stay in the lorry. He warned me not to leave the lorry until he said the word. I had no idea where I was. I didn't dare to ask the driver. He set off down the road.

*   *   *

I participated actively in the house church once a week, usually at six on Wednesday evenings, or on Sundays after my work. I was a primary school teacher in Shahr-e Ray or Ray, the oldest existing city in Tehran province of Iran.

Ray had been subject to severe destruction during the successive medieval invasions of the Arabs, Turks, and Mongols. It had also been home to many historical figures such as Reza Shah of the Pahlavi dynasty, who was buried in a mausoleum in this city. Naser al-Din Shah Qajar of Persia was also buried in Shah Abdol-Azim shrine, a revered Shia pilgrim site in Ray. Abu Bakr Muhammad ibn Zakariya al-Razi (Latin Rhazes), a celebrated Persian physician, alchemist and Muslim philosopher, was from this city.

It took me nearly two hours to get to the house church. I was first connected to this place by Arbi, my student's father, who was a Christian from birth. He earned his living as a fishmonger in Tehran. During our friendship, he had realised that I had started to no longer believe in Allah and so, as a friend he wanted to help me find my way in life spiritually. He gradually started talking to me about Christianity. He gave me a Bible. He acquainted me with the four Gospels and the teachings of Jesus Christ.

"Why are you always cranky?" he would ask.

"I'm absolutely knackered," I used to answer.

I worked five days a week at school. The job was a sort of shelter for me. It took me away from my troubles. Working for children was a blessing. Time moved very quickly at school. But outside my work I was a different person. I was reticent, irritable, droopy, and always tired. To me it seemed my lack of devotion and faith in God was the reason for all my miseries. Gradually being with the house church changed my outlook and my mood towards life. A smile returned to my lips.

I was very happy with Arbi. I saw comfort and joy in his character. His words and behaviour gave solace to my heart. Arbi encouraged me to attend the Alpha courses, whose purpose was to introduce the basics of the Christian faith and Christ's teachings through a series of talks and discussions. In Iran, however, such courses and gatherings were forbidden, so they are held in private homes, and in secret. Arbi knew a priest who was leading the church services.

The priest first taught me a couple of security and safety measures to better protect the congregation. For example, it was necessary to come separately, not in a group, in order to avoid suspicion, and to not carry the Bible or other holy books to the house church, and to gather for meetings in different places.

We started with a prayer, then a couple of songs such as "Holy, holy, holy! Lord God Almighty," in English with Persian translation. When we finished the songs, he read a few pages from Bible. The priest asked questions and we answered. At the end we had coffee and biscuits. There was always one of us to care for the service respectively. This person should be punctual. Preparing coffee and tea, giving out Bibles, and controlling our arrivals and exits were all part of his or her duties.

CHAPTER 3

It was pouring down all day. I got soaked. The blanket could not protect me from the rain. It was 12 March 2018 in the afternoon, and the driver had been driving nonstop for two days. It was getting colder. My wet clothes intensified the chilliness. The driver sometimes drove up and sometimes down the road. I still felt scared. My health was hugely impacted both physically and mentally. My body began to ache. My leg was numb. I felt pins and needles from my sciatica. I had had sciatica and backpain for nearly three years, but previously they were not a big issue. This journey aggravated my conditions. Before midnight the lorry stopped. The driver removed the blanket and said, "Hop out of the lorry. We must walk from here." Then we trekked continuously through forests and over hills for approximately three hours nonstop, until we arrived at a cottage in a small village. At first, I thought it felt a threat, but later I found out it was a secure place. There were only two or three houses in that spot which were very distant from each other. Each surrounded by lots of trees.

I didn't trust the driver. There was something creepy about the way he looked at me. His looks were ghastly. I could hardly breathe, and my heart was beating fast. My hands began to shake. *If he happened to assault me, I wouldn't be able to defend myself,* I thought. It was absolutely dark. There was no one in the village. It seemed deserted, with no light, no sound, only an eerie silence. Time seemed to stop.

The cottage was surrounded by thick trees and shrubs. At night these appeared like a group of staring people.

The driver pointed towards the door of the cottage. The house looked abandoned and gloomy. It was filled with dust, cobwebs, spiders, centipedes, and many other insects I couldn't recognize. The curtains were dirty and ripped. There was a two-seated red sofa and a small rug in the sitting room. The house had three rooms one of which was furnished with a single bed. The kitchen had a fridge and a cooker.

The driver gave me a bag. "You should stay here for a few days until my colleague comes to you. Never ever leave the cottage and never open the door to anyone," he said.

"How long will I be here?" I said, feeling scared and nervous.

"I have no idea, but I'll drop by here occasionally to bring you some food." Then he left.

I had no idea where I was. I was cut from the outside world. There was no internet, and I had no sim card in my mobile phone. I was worried about my family. Before I left my friend Armin in Iran, I begged him to contact my family to see how they were. He had promised to do so.

Has Armin called my parents? Are they getting along well? I wondered. I struggled to sleep but I couldn't.

It was cold about midnight. The wind was whispering. I could hear the howling of wolves. The lights in the sitting room were flickering. The gate was creaking. The house smelled damp and moulding. The haunting atmosphere gave me a sense of horror. I felt surrounded by spooky objects, spectral shadows, and figures, which seemed to be sneering and glaring at my miseries with rage and hate. I also feared that someone might come through the window or open the door. The setting reminded me of the isolated cabin in *'I Spit on Your Grave.'* Jennifer, a writer, rented a cabin so that she could work on her novel but the peace and quiet was shattered by a gang of local thugs.

In the morning I went to the window. It was raining. No one could be seen near the cottage. I could see only the garden. It was untidy and the plants were untrimmed as if it had been deserted for a long time.

I looked around closely to see if I could find something to entertain myself such as a book to read or anything that could help me pass the time or as a way to distract me for a time from the miseries I was in. Unfortunately, I saw nothing of the sort. It was really devastating.

Sometimes, I felt I was *'Cast Away'* like Chuck Nolan who was marooned on a desolate island after he had a deadly plane crash. With no way to escape, Chuck had to find ways to survive in his new home. Never before had I thought of myself as being trapped in a situation like that. I had always thought that there would always be a way to survive the difficulties and hardships in life. One had to get prepared for any unwelcome events so I tried to collect myself to see what I could do.

To calm myself, I tried to pray. I racked my brains to remember a song we used to sing in the house church:

> King of kings
> In the darkness
> We were waiting
> Without hope
> Without light
> Till from heaven
> You came running
> There was mercy
> In your eyes
> To fulfil the law and prophets
> To a virgin came the world
> From a throne of endless glory
> To a cradle in the dirt
> Praise the Father,
> Praise the son
> Praise the spirit
> Three in one.
> Glory of glory
> Majesty
> Praise forever to the
> King
> Of
> Kings.

When I finished singing the song, I began to feel better. I was no longer alone. I could see God's presence with me. I entreated God to help me get out of this situation and to find a safe place. I also begged him to protect my family.

CHAPTER 4

The second day of my stay in this cottage passed the same as the day before. The driver turned up only twice to hand over food and water. When I asked him when the smuggler would come, he just said, "I have no idea. Just wait, he'll appear." Later I asked him to bring me a pack of cigarettes, but he didn't give a damn.

On the fourth day, as I was cooking something to eat, I heard two or three people walking by the gate. I was unable to hear them clearly, but it seemed they were speaking Turkish. It occurred to me that they were probably non-Iranians because I could see one of the men. He was short and fat. He was wearing Turkish traditional dress—a white shirt, a red vest, red baggy pants, and a red Turkish hat or Fez. Now I was quite sure I was somewhere in Turkey.

About a week passed but there was still no news from the smuggler. He didn't appear until the eleventh day of my stay at the cottage. It was terrifying to be left alone in such a hopeless condition, not knowing what was happening and what was awaiting me.

It was early morning about six. Heavy fog made it very difficult to see outside the windows. He opened the door with the key he had. I was astonished at seeing a tall, handsome guy about thirty. *Very young for such a job,* I thought. "You can call me Omid," he said.

He asked me to get ready for the journey. He explained all the things I needed to know. He asked me to be less talkative, to smile always, to feel relaxed, and to not stay away from him. He looked strict but didn't make me feel uncomfortable. I tried to trust him. I couldn't think differently. The smuggler showed me an envelope and told me that it contained my passport. But he warned me not to open it for security reasons except when the officer at the airport asked me to see my passport.

Why should I not see the passport? I thought. This frightened me so much.

We left the cottage and walked for about thirty minutes along narrow, uneven paths until we reached a wider road, where his black van was parked.

"There's no need to hide yourself in the car or anywhere from now on. We are in Turkey," he said.

I was able to see the area in daylight. The car passed through a forest, then an astounding lake.

The smuggler drove for nearly four hours nonstop on a motorway. Then we arrived in a big city and stopped across the road from a shopping centre. He advised me not to leave the car while he went inside the shopping centre. That day I felt confident that I was in Turkey because I could see many Turkish flags, banners and placards on the walls and lamp posts with pictures of the Turkish president, Tayyip Erdogan.

After nearly half an hour, Omid, the smuggler, came back with a large paper bag and handed it over to me.

"Your current clothes are not appropriate for your destination. You need proper attire," he said with a friendly grin on his face.

"I'm really grateful to you, but I'm still so scared." I groaned in disappointment. *I wouldn't believe I could pass this stage*, I thought.

"Don't worry. You're going to be alright. You just need to show the pass and tickets and then go aboard the plane. I'll come after you. We'll meet at the airport," murmured Omid. He didn't give any more explanations about the journey. I waited with dismay for his signal to set off for airport.

CHAPTER 5

We arrived at the airport around midday. My heart started racing, and I began to feel lightheaded and slightly queasy. *What will become of me if I was caught?* I wondered.

The flight was at 13:10 and I had only one hour to wait before the flight. I found a vacant seat. I was extremely knackered, and my body was aching. For a few seconds I thought I was going to blackout. I felt my anxiety was intensifying as the time for the flight approached.

To calm myself down, I started praying.

I should concentrate on the journey, or I'll ruin my only chance of escape, I said to myself.

I looked for the smuggler, but I couldn't see him. I remembered he had told me he'd arrive after me.

I looked at my watch. It was time to go to the check-in counter. I had my luggage tagged. The smuggler had given me a small suitcase and told me to carry it with me to avoid suspicion. The bag intensified my worries because I didn't have any idea what he might have put in it.

Then I passed through the security checkpoint. My pass and boarding pass were checked. My luggage went into the x-ray machine. I had to remove all metallic objects and shoes and put them on the belt.

This was the most critical and hazardous part of the journey. I just prayed and tried to relax. I tried to avoid giving any indications of fear or worry.

"Business or pleasure?" the security officer asked.

"Pleasure Sir," I replied.

"Any friends or relatives over there?"

"No sir. Nobody sir," I replied.

"What is your profession?"

"I'm a teacher."

"What do you teach?"

"English."

The officer handed the passport over to me and told me to proceed.

"Enjoy your journey,"

"Thank you."

I couldn't believe my eyes. What a relief! I could hardly express the joy I felt at this time. But I was still worried and scared because I thought the security offices at the airport might find out about my true identity or that I was holding a fake passport.

Where is Omid, the smuggler? I looked for him everywhere at the airport, but I couldn't see him. He must have gone to ground. Panic began to grip me. Why did he leave me? Was he caught by the police? If so, what would become of me? Would they learn that I was with him? I couldn't get those questions out of my head

Feeling hopeless and miserable, I went to board the plane. He never came.

CHAPTER 6

The plane landed in London about 5 pm. I couldn't believe that the smuggler got me here. I could remember Armin had asked him to take me out of the country when we found out my life was in danger. We feared that plain-clothes police were lying in ambush waiting to arrest us. So we agreed that there was only one option for me and that was to disappear without a trace.

In Iran, according to Islamic laws, conversion to other religions is considered a sin and a Muslim must be aware of it. A person who becomes Christian is called an apostate and the punishment for such people is at least long-term imprisonment. It is a betrayal of one's religion. The restrictions and new regulations haven't had a deterrent effect on the people who are interested to experience other religions and new outlook. Today the number of house churches all over the country is increasing. They gather with family members or with friends in small groups. New Christians share their new faith with each other. Prayer and Bible reading are part of their main practises. Some house churches have ministers who handle the courses and teachings whilst others go online or have internet pastors.

Iranian authorities find the house churches movement a threat against national security. House church gatherings are held in secret accordingly. This means the government can neither control who participates nor what happens in the meetings. The government consider the Christian movement to be a source of threat to the whole system or regime. But, in fact, house church attenders never talked about politics and didn't attend any political opposition activities. We just regularly met once a week for prayer, singing, Bible reading and collection. House churches collected money from members only for charitable work.

I waited for hours for the smuggler to appear, but he didn't. I thought he might join me at the airport. I had no documents to present if police asked me to. I remember he had grabbed my passport as soon as I received my boarding pass in Turkey. He told me he would come back to me very soon.

How ghastly! How very very awful! I thought.

My feeling of terror was growing. My heart began beating fast. The thought of having to face police or airport security staff filled me with anxiety.

When I feel anxious and stressful, I start having trouble concentrating, my body trembles, and sweat streams down my forehead. As a result, I need to rest or lie down for a few seconds so that I can regain my strength and vigour.

CHAPTER 7

After many attempts to see where the smuggler had been, I finally gave up and approached one of the airport officers.

"I want to claim asylum," I said.

I felt deeply ashamed that I was situated in such an inferior position. I also felt wretched not knowing what reactions I would receive from the security officers, since I had no papers to present showing who I was.

A security officer led me towards an escalator, I followed him downstairs. He then directed me to a counter. A girl was at the desk checking papers.

"Another asylum seeker!" he said. The girl opened a small, tinted glass gate. We followed her into a room which was exactly behind the counter. She asked me to be seated.

"What's your full name?" she asked politely.

"Cyrus Aryani." My voice trembled as I began to speak.

"What's your country of origin?"

"Iran."

"Your passport please!"

"I don't have my passport. The smuggler took it from me and didn't return it. He vanished. I have been waiting here for a couple of hours."

"I don't find his name on the flight list," she said to the man.

The man took out a few papers from drawers and asked me to complete them. The girl took a photo of me and then measured my height and weight. Finally, I had my biometrics recorded— fingerprints and facial image.

It was nearly 11:00 pm, on the 22nd of March. The airport was eerily empty and quiet, with most of the concourse lights turned off. Heathrow, the busiest airport in the United Kingdom, was closed for the night, as no flights were permitted to take off or land between 11:30 pm and 6:00 am.

For the asylum claim, there were other formalities to be completed and further enquiries to be made. I was said that I was liable to be detained so I was taken to a place to stay the night at the airport. It felt like a prison. I had never been into a prison, but I had seen them in films and on TV, and I didn't see much difference. That was my first time in my life that I had been in a setting like this. It was quite distressing. The room was small. The light was poor. There was only one window which was adjacent to an office, overlooking the room from which immigration officers and security staff could watch us. There was a small table in the centre and a small bookcase under the window. A bed which I was supposed to sleep on was exactly opposite the toilet.

I was gripped by fear at my first sight of the room. Being held in such a ghastly, creepy place was tremendously frightening. I wondered how long they were going to keep me here! That was very disappointing.

There were two people working at the desk. One of them later came into my room.

"Would you like to have something to eat?" he asked.

"Yes please. I'm very hungry."

"We have chicken and bacon pasta, tomato and mozzarella pasta bake, beef lasagne, and shepherd's pie. Which do you prefer?"

"Shepherd's pie please."

When he returned, he put the food and a drink on the table and left.

After I had my food, I tried to sleep as I was feeling out of sorts and completely drained of energy.

CHAPTER 8

"Wake up Mr Cyrus Aryani. You have an interview right now," said the security staff.

"Can you please make it in the morning? It's 2:30 am. Too early. I need to rest."

I felt it was totally unfair to wake up an asylum seeker like me at this hour.

"If you do not attend the Home Office interview, your application for asylum will be considered as withdrawn and steps will be made to remove you from the UK."

I went after him despite my pleadings to be allowed to stay in my bed. We walked for a few minutes until we arrived at a room.

It was a tiny, dark room at the end of a narrow corridor. When I stepped inside, I saw two people sitting on one side of a table. There was an empty chair on the other side which was to be taken by me.

I wondered what lay ahead of me. The idea of going to jail was frightful. I felt myself to be in a helpless, defenceless condition.

What if they would send me back to Iran. There was an ominous silence before they start. It was giving me the jitters. One of them started with an accent that I could not fully understand. It struck me that she was originally from South Asia.

"I am Maliha Aqidah. I'm going to interview you as part of your application," she said in a harsh and menacing tone.

"Do you require an interpreter?"

"Yes please," I said in a trembling low voice.

Due to frustration, lack of concentration, and dizziness, resulting from panic and misgivings, I thought it would be better to have a Farsi interpreter.

"I'm going to ask you some questions about your identity, family, travel history, and some health and welfare questions," she said. "I will only ask you for a brief outline of why you are claiming asylum. I may not be the person who makes the decision on your asylum claim."

"As you are applying for asylum, you must apply for a Biometric Residence Permit (BRP) since, if you are granted permission to live in the UK, you will need one," she added.

The interview started around 2:45 am. I was bombarded by far too many questions, and all without a break. The interviewer did not care how I was feeling. She just wanted to do her duty — in other words, it was a just another task to be checked off her day's to-do-list. There was no smile on her face as if she was questioning someone distasteful, or a criminal. When she came to the section of questions related to religion, her tone became harsh and menacing.

"What is your religion?"

"Christian. I am a protestant. I converted from Islam."

"Is that the reason for claiming asylum?"

"Yes, it is."

"You all say the same thing. You come to the UK and say, "I converted to Christianity," or "I became a gay," but only with the intention of claiming for asylum?

"Why does she speak like that?" I asked the interpreter in Farsi, to explain to the interviewer what she meant by posing such a question. "It is not professional or even right to speak to me this way. I am knackered, vulnerable, and helpless," I said. "Could you please tell her that she is disrespecting and humiliating me, and what she says is not true?"

"Sorry I didn't mean to hurt you." The interviewer apologised for her words. Her voice was softer now.

The interview lasted for around three hours. I was taken back to the room I had first come from. I felt distraught at the way the interview was held. Why did I take such offence when the interviewer said, "You all say the same thing?" I shouldn't have talked back to her that way I did. I panicked, and for a moment, I thought I was going to black out.

I kept imagining the door opening and a security officer coming in to arrest me. The thought of deportation terrified me. I struggled to fall sleep that night.

When I woke up, I noticed a couple of new asylum seekers with their children, lying down on the floor. Their luggage was scattering around in the room.

All were sleeping. I later learnt they were from many countries and different continents: African, Asian, and east Europe. They all looked very tired. Weary. They must have had a long, terrible journey or had been through a lot of unpleasant experiences. I could see it on their faces, and from their clothes, and snores. *They were lucky that they had finally reached the UK, their destination,* I thought.

I later discovered more and more miseries that asylum seekers had encountered before entering the UK. As I was in a hostel in Derby, I had an opportunity to listen to some of the asylum seekers who shared their frightful stories with me. The reasons why they had left their hometowns, or their countries were many and varied.

Many of these asylum seekers were from Iran, Iraq, Albania, Sudan, Syria, Yemen, Somalia, Eritrea, and Ethiopia. They fled war, or persecution, in their home country, trying to find a safe place where they could rebuild their lives.

After lunch, one of the immigration securities informed me that I should collect my things and get ready to leave the airport.

"Will you please tell me where we are going?" I asked. Worry and fear returned to me.

"I have no idea Sir," he answered. I suspected he knew the answer but wasn't allowed to disclose it.

CHAPTER 9

At 5:00 pm, 23 March, it was finally time to be off. And I left.

There were nine of us with our things. We followed a driver into a parking area, where two vans were waiting for us. Inside the van I felt a glimmer of hope because there were no police or immigration security staff with us. In fact, we were left unattended. I felt sort of relaxed, knowing I was not alone, but among asylum seekers.

At 8:00 pm, the same day, we arrived at a hotel in Croydon, South London.

The hotel had more than twenty small rooms. Every one of us shared a room with two or three other people. My room was on the third floor. Our meals were served on the ground floor on a strict schedule. On my first day, I was late for breakfast and by the time I arrived, there was nothing for me to eat. I found out that I should have been downstairs before 10 am. So I went hungry the whole day. I didn't have enough money to buy something to eat elsewhere.

I was surprised that we had the permission to stay outside the hotel for a time, but it was until evening. I saw some of the asylum seekers leaving the hotel. *How delightful freedom is!*

There was a church close to the hotel. I went there to see if I could get some help. It was Sunday and, though the services hadn't started yet, the church was very crowded. I was very delighted to be at a church in England for the first time of my life. After the service, I talked to the pastor whose name was Stephen King. He welcomed me with open arms.

"Would you like to pray for you?"

"Yes please, with pleasure."

He then touched my shoulder and started praying.

He gave me a Bible as a gift and a £50.00 note. "You are Jesus Christ's guest. Please let me know if you need any help."

"Thanks a lot. I just needed some money to buy a sim card. I haven't talked with my parents yet."

CHAPTER 10

After church, I went to a supermarket and bought a Sim card.

"Hey mom. How are you?"

My mom was too excited to talk.

"Cyrus." It was all she could say before bursting into tears. She begged me to take care of myself.

"I'm fine. Things are looking up, mom. Don't worry about me."

"You mean you're not going to be deported?"

"No, not at all. How's dad? Where's he?"

"He's in bed, sleeping. His condition is the same."

"No change?"

"Don't worry. He'll be fine.

"Tell Bardia to take dad to his doctor."

Bardia was my younger brother. From the time I left Iran, he had been looking after our parents. He did shopping for them, took Dad to his doctor, and checked his diabetes. Bardia was kind and reliable and I could always count on him to do what he had promised.

"Ok, where are you now?" asked my mother.

"I'm in London, in a hotel."

"Are you comfortable there? Do they serve food?"

"Yes, mom. I'm very grateful to all those who are caring for us."

"I pray for those who were so generous to you. By the way, two plain-clothes police officers came here after you left Iran. They wanted to know your whereabouts."

23

"Didn't they hurt you? What happened then?

"One of them went upstairs without our permission to investigate."

"Did they take my laptop?"

"No, I had put it in a safe place after Armin called us to be aware and cautious. But they took a few books and left.

"Don't worry, they can't touch me," I said. "Ok mom, I must go now. We'll talk later. Take care."

CHAPTER 11

I had two roommates, a Syrian and a Russian.

Rahman, the Syrian, was about 28 years old. He was a handsome guy, reticent but polite. The following day we went outside together for a walk around the hotel, not too far, to kill time and to forget our troubles for a while.

After I shared some of the troubles I had encountered on my journey, Rahman felt comfortable to confide in me and he told me the spooky story of his own journey.

"We were four of us. Two boys from Afghanistan, and an Iraqi man. Bulgarian border guards found us while we were making our way from Turkey to Bulgaria. We were in detention for five days in a city in Bulgaria, near Turkey. We were forced to undress. They stripped us of our money and our belongings. When the Iraqi objected to them why they took away his mobile phone, they started to beat him violently. We were without food the whole day. The detention centre looked old, gloomy, and filthy. It was somewhere far from the city. Every day they looked for an excuse to treat us violently, beating us with fists, batons, or kicks. On the fifth day we were taken back to Turkey."

When Pavel, my Russian roommate, realised that I had purchased a sim card, he asked me to lend him my cell phone. He wanted to talk to his friends. I thought I should help him since we were all in the same boat, alone, forlorn, and needy. His call lasted about half an hour. The next day he came to me again and demanded to give him my mobile.

"I see you have more than 200 dollars. Why don't you use your own mobile phone? Buy a sim card and top it up." Although he had enough money, it seemed he didn't want to spend it.

"Just lend it to me one last time." He was infuriated by my words.

"That's ok. Just five minutes." I was getting scared of his aggressive behaviour.

"I need the money." He talked to me at the top of his voice.

"I am not responsible for your expenses. I thought you were needy and helpless," I replied in a low voice.

Rahman overheard us while we were arguing.

"Yesterday you asked me to give you £30 while I see you are richer than a king." He turned to Pavel and said, "We are not in the money. Understand?"

After breakfast, I went back to the church to see the pastor, but he was not there. A couple of church members were doing a charity work, helping needy and vulnerable people. One of the church members approached.

"When can I see Fr Stephen?" I asked.

"He'll be back in two weeks. He's outside the UK, doing some missionary work," she replied.

"Can I have his number?" I asked, "I'm leaving London today."

After I got Fr Stephen's number, I left the church.

I wandered around the street leading to the hotel. I went up to my room to pack my things.

No one had any idea what time we were to leave the hotel. All asylum seekers were ready with their luggage in the hall. Some were getting restless including me. Nervous because we didn't really know where they were going to take us. The unknown was creating fear in me, aggravating my conditions. My right leg started to go numb. I worried that when it came time to go, I would barely be able to walk. I went outside to the front yard where there were some tables with chairs.

I remained seated until a coach came. The driver had a list. He called our names and asked us to get on the bus. It took 45 minutes before we were ready to set off.

"Some of you go to Derby, some to Sheffield and some Leeds," he said.

I felt totally drained both physically and mentally, and so, once in my seat, I dropped off quickly and slept like a log. When I woke up, two or three hours had passed. The coach was on a motorway.

Then the coach driver suddenly stopped somewhere. He took a piece of paper out of his pocket and began to read.

"The names I read, they'll go to Derby. These people should leave the bus. There's a van outside to take you to a hostel in Derby. Others should stay on the bus."

My name was in the Derby list, so I left the bus. There were nine of us in my group.

After half an hour's drive, we arrived at a hostel in Derby.

CHAPTER 12

I was filled with gloom as I arrived at the hostel. I looked around. It was raining. A heavy mass of grey cloud was creeping across the sky. The yard was almost empty. I saw only two or three guys in the distant, going into one of the buildings. I felt as though I had been sent to an uninhabited, deserted place. I also got disappointed and scared when I saw the state of the buildings inside the hostel, the iron gate and the security office adjoining it.

The hostel was located close to the city centre. I first thought they would take us to a remote area, far from citizens, and would treat us like prisoners. But it was the other way around. The hostel was surrounded by houses, shops, and there was even a primary school within 5 minutes walking distance.

We waited in the yard next to the security office, responsible for monitoring comings and goings, until a bearded man approached.

"Welcome to the Derby hostel. I'm Ahmed, one of the security staff. Before sending you to your rooms I'll give you an induction briefing first. I try to familiarise you with the rules of the hostel."

He talked for an hour about emergency, times of leaving and returning, and proper asylum seeker behaviour— courteous, disciplined, and good personal hygiene. He then gave us time to pose questions.

"How long are we going to stay here?" an asylum seeker asked.

"Your stay at this hostel is temporary. It might be about twenty days

28

until your claim for asylum support is assessed. Then you would move into Dispersed Accommodation," he replied with a big smile.

"What about our daily expenses, for example buying food, clothes, mobile contacts or any other costs?" asked Rahman, the Syrian man, whom I had shared a room with earlier.

"Whilst you are in this centre, you are fully supported, including having access to voluntary sector organizations and health services. Each asylum seeker receives a daily payment of £5.00 per day for subsistence or livelihood. It's minimal, so it will only enable you to buy basic goods such as food or clothing."

"What happens next?" I asked.

"After your stay at this hostel ends, you will be dispersed to different locations. At this stage, asylum seekers will remain in the new accommodations while their claim for asylum is being assessed by the Home Office. Once their claim has been assessed, decisions can include positive leave to remain or negative refusal. Asylum seekers then are asked to leave the Dispersed Accommodation," he explained.

At the end of the induction briefing, he told us that we must sign a daily register and return to the hostel by 10 pm. We followed him into our rooms. We had been assigned to different buildings. The hostel consisted of half a dozen three-story buildings. Each floor had a TV room and a kitchen fully equipped with a big fridge, dishwasher, washing machine and a stove. The hostel was self-catered, and facilities were provided for cooking. Toilets and showers were next to the kitchen at the end of the corridor.

My room was on the second floor overlooking the yard. There were three of us assigned together. A young, heavy-set boy about 24 years old was on one bed talking on his mobile, and another guy, whose face I couldn't see, lying down on another bed. All three of us fidgeting. Idle.

That night, as I was very tired, I went to bed at about 9 pm. I was sleeping soundly and peacefully when a sudden loud noise woke me up. I saw two young people enter the room and go towards my roommate. They started talking loudly with each other. I wanted to ask them to leave the room and talk outside or at least to be quieter, but I decided not to intervene. I didn't know these people and it was my first night, so I didn't want to get involved in a dispute. Instead, I just covered my head with the duvet. I realised that I was going to have a very difficult time ahead.

Next morning, I woke up and left the room. First, I went downstairs to the security office and registered my name, as we had been advised to do so at the induction briefing. Then I returned to my room to prepare myself for breakfast. In the kitchen I met a couple of asylum seekers who were having breakfast. The kitchen was at the end of the corridor next to the TV room.

"Hi, how's it going? I'm Yonas from Eritrea," said the young guy who was making tea.

"Fine, thanks," I said then I introduced myself to him.

"I see you've just come to this hostel."

"Yes, yesterday evening."

He told me that he had been here for two months, waiting for an answer from Home Office.

"How long are we going to stay at this hostel?" I asked.

"No one knows. One of my roommates left the hostel three weeks after he came. Another guy has been here for four months waiting to receive a dispersal letter," he added.

After I had my breakfast, I went back to my room. I saw both roommates on their beds, one appeared to be sleeping.

"Hi. I'm Cyrus. What's your name?"

"Hi I'm Aras."

His English was not good. He spoke with difficulty, and with a Kurdish accent. Aras was from Sulaymaniyah, a city in the east of the Kurdish region of Iraq. He left Iraq because his life was in danger. He was reluctant to share his story with me, so I didn't press him. He was full of energy and seemed to have known many people, never leaving the hostel alone. During the day Aras would hang around with his friends who were mostly from Kurdistan, and at night he would chat on his mobile with his family. Sometimes his friends joined him in our room. They were all boisterous like Aras. Honestly, I was not able to sleep during the night for they met in our room and would talk at the top of their voices. One night I was fast asleep when the door was suddenly pushed open. One of Aras's friends bumped into my bed violently and gave me a big jolt. They turned on the light and started a loud conversation.

"What are you doing? Can't you see I am trying to sleep?" I was infuriated at their rudeness and asked them to leave the room.

One of them apologised and left, but the other remained and continued talking with Aras. They didn't care about me or about what I said.

CHAPTER 13

The next day I was in the kitchen having my breakfast by myself. The door opened gently, and I saw the manager of the hostel.

I was surprised to see her at the kitchen early in the morning. She was a beautiful blond-haired woman in her mid-sixties, kind and very responsive to the needs and problems of asylum seekers. I would always see her in the yard exchanging greetings with everyone. She listened to all the problems of the asylum seekers, and always tried to give the best guidance she could. I hadn't heard anything unpleasant about her character.

"Hi darling. How's it going?" she said with a big smile.

Hi. I'm fine." I returned her smile warmly.

"Does anything worry you?" she asked.

"Will you please do me a favour?" I responded.

"What is it? I will if I can!"

"I am not alright in my room. My roommate is young, with many young, boisterous friends, full of life as is their nature at their age. But they routinely come into our shared room and keep me awake during the night. I am 54 and I need rest. I need to go to sleep early, or sometimes to read something in peace. I need to be in a quiet place of my own. They're nice people but I cannot live with them."

"What type of books do you read?" She inquired, looking curious about what I am interested in.

"Literature and history."

"Wow! Look at that! My daughter has studied English literature too," she said, "My parents named me after a writer who wrote 'The Garden Party.' Can you guess who she is if you know literature?" she asked me with a laugh. It felt she wished to make me feel happy by posing this question.

"She is Catherine Mansfield. I've read the story. I like it."

"Well done! Ok I'll help you with this. What's your name?"

"Thank you so much. I appreciate that. Anyway, I'm Cyrus Aryani."

"I have a vacant room tomorrow, so pack your stuff and come to the security office tomorrow."

Catherine really made my day. She was an angel.

That night I could sleep well despite my roommate and his friends' inconsiderate noises. I remained still, not moving a muscle.

The next morning, I moved to my new single room, in another building. I was finally completely by myself, with nothing or no one to disturb me. In my small room, I had a table and a chair, a basin in one corner and a cupboard with shelves to keep dishes and utensils.

In the communal kitchen I met Siavash, an Iranian journalist who lived in the next room. He was a short, fat man with little hair on his head, aged about 47, from Shiraz, a city in south-central Iran. He had started his career writing articles for a local newspaper, Ayandeh, meaning Future. He was forced to flee the country at the beginning of 2018. Siavash was given a ten-year prison sentence for writing articles supporting public protests that took place in Iran in 2017-2018.

CHAPTER 14

I attended an English class twice a week and Alpha three times a week with other asylum seekers, including Siavash. We gathered in the yard next to the security office an hour before the start of each class. We were a group of men and women from different countries, three of whom were from Iran. I used the English class with the intention of improving my English and to learn the methods teachers used in teaching.

These classes were free for asylum seekers. Jason was a fabulous teacher who managed his class very well. He was one of the best English teachers I had ever seen. His class was very active. Everyone was given the opportunity to express their opinions and feelings. It was not just an English class. It was also a psychology class. Jason taught us how to face or cope with problems in our new society as an asylum seeker. Jason's class was in fact a life class. We also learned from each other in regard to our culture, history, and literature, as the class consisted of people from a variety of different nations. We all came to the UK with similar objectives, to begin a journey into a new world that was previously unknown to us.

There seemed to be a sense of confusion and uncertainty, with feelings of anxiety that could impact asylum seekers who were exposed to a foreign culture — a culture shock. In other words, we all had fear of not being accepted or of being looked or treated as an outsider.

Mixing with other nations was another major issue caused by language barrier. So, to proceed properly and find our social status in the society, one must put a lot of effort into it. It is not easy, but it is worth the effort.

The flip side of that coin is the excitement and great joy which comes from the unknown. There is ecstasy in learning new things, facing new challenges, a variety of religions, and plenty of tastes and styles and languages. All these provide a great stimulus to keep on.

At break, which lasted about twenty minutes, we had the opportunity to socialise and mix with students while having coffee in the hall.

We also attended Bible study classes, another interesting and useful gathering which was led by Jonathan in his own home. In this class only Iranians took part, and we had an interpreter since not all of us knew English well enough.

At every session a reflective question was posed for group discussion. For example, "Has Jesus touched you in any discernible way this week?" or "Have you ever seen or felt Christ's power in your life?" We would all discuss this together, sharing our personal thoughts and experiences. We would then read parts of Bible together. We would pray together, for ourselves, for our families, and for those we knew living in desperate conditions. Finally, one by one, each approached Jonathan and asked him to pray for us individually.

Jonathan was a tall, good-looking man in his fifties. His positive traits were his smiles, his patience, and his listening ears—his sympathetic ear. He was a minister who devoted his life to evangelising people. I first met him at a church in Derby. I always remember the way he said a prayer for me and for others after the service. Jonathan grasped our hands, closed his eyes and then prayed for us for four or five minutes each without rushing. Everyone received or at least felt comfort and energy that we had not previously experienced. His smile, while praying, was curious. He devoted himself fully to serve Jesus Christ.

Before the Iranian Revolution in 1978-1979, Jonathan had travelled to Iran as part of his missionary work. He taught people about Christianity and sought to persuade them to become Christians. He had also served in Afghanistan, India, and China. He told us that he didn't receive any money for his missionary work, and he only did it for the love of Jesus Christ. I participated in all his sessions until I was dispersed to Middlesbrough, another city in the north of England.

Most of the asylum seekers left Derby to other cities, many of whom were taken to north.

Derby is a city in Derbyshire, England. At the beginning, Derby was a market town. It grew rapidly in the field of industry. The Silk Mill was built in the 18th century by John Lombe, a silk spinner, in Derby. Railways came to the city in the 19th century. The Rolls Royce factory is a famous place for tourists to visit, with other sites such as the Cathedral Church of All Saints. The Derby Museum and Art Gallery is home to Joseph Wright paintings.

CHAPTER 15

In Derby, I was introduced to a lady who ran an allotment. Her name was Elizabeth. She was a blonde, good-hearted woman in her late seventies. She had rented the land to grow her own fruits and vegetables, but she told us that most of the produce actually went to charity. There were five or six of us from the hostel who volunteered to work at the allotment, where I met Elizabeth. We worked once a week, for four or five hours. It was my favourite and most enjoyable pastime during my stay in Derby.

At the allotment we learned how to grow fruit and vegetables from seeds, and how to protect plants before harvest. The reason why we accepted the work was to, sort of, show our sincere thankfulness and appreciation to the UK for accommodating us, protecting us, and letting us, as asylum seekers, achieve our goals. It was the least we could do to express our gratitude.

At the allotment, we sang songs while working. I remember I once started singing the Beatle's songs, "Yellow Submarine." Elizabeth joined in with me, upon heard me singing the song. In turn, we also began to sing a Persian song. We enjoyed working, since it was fun for us. At break, we had coffee and biscuits that Elizabeth routinely brought. When we finished our work, she would let us pick flowers, vegetables, and fruits.

We helped Elizabeth at the allotment for nearly two months, until we each left Derby one by one.

Once a week, several new asylum seekers would arrive at the hostel and approximately the same number would depart. Departing from hostel was an encouraging step, one that gave everyone hope towards their own promising future. We would all be delighted to see the name of a friend appear on the list, which was pinned to a bulletin board, usually the night before the lucky person's departure. We often went to the security office to have a look at the board to see whose turn it was to leave the hostel. If it happened to one of our friends, we would tap excitedly on their door or call out to the fortunate one with joy, to celebrate him or her together in the happy news. It was more than two months before I received my own such call.

"Hi Cyrus. Where are you?" She was Niloofar, one of the girls who came with us to the Bible study. She was young, pretty, with long dark hair. Her voice was light and pleasant. In Iran she had been studying medicine, in her third year. She was forced to leave the country due to violent threats by her husband. Niloofar's husband had not given her permission to study at university. She had enrolled at university anyway, after which they started to have big arguments. He would often beat her during these, and one day he became so angry that he threatened that he would throw acid on her if she persisted. Fearing for her safety, she left her home while her husband was at work. She went to stay at a friend's house for several days, and then with the help of her parents she fled, first to Turkey, and from there to the UK.

When Niloofar found out that I was in my room, she came and knocked on my door. When I opened the door, I noted that she looked prettier than ever. She was wearing a red top with a blue skirt and a pair of white sandals.

"Hi Niloofar. You look very happy today."

"I have good news for you. Guess what?"

"Is it my turn to depart?"

"Yes! Bull's eye! Your name is on the list. Time to pack your stuff."

I leapt with joy into the air by the news.

"Thanks a million, Niloofar. I hope next time will be your turn very soon."

"Cheers! See you tomorrow morning."

Before she turned to leave, I gave her a gentle kiss on the cheek, instinctively. A waft of exotic perfume lingered in the air, as she departed.

In the evening, I packed my things first, and then I went to the security office to see my name on the list with my own eyes. It was true. There were six people on the list, and mine was second.

We usually gathered in the yard and had our dinner together. This was our routine. Our dinner would turn into a goodbye party, however, whenever we learned that one of us was going to leave the hostel. This time it was my turn. Some friends brought beer and crisps, at their own expense. It was 8 pm when I left my room, and I found a couple of friends waiting for me. They all shouted together, "Hip, hip, hurray!" Then Ahmad, a Syrian boy who had recently arrived, put on "Jaybli Salam" from Fairuz, a Lebanese singer. She is considered by many as one of the leading vocalists and most famous singers in the history of the Arab world. She is also known as "the Soul of Lebanon." This song was followed by many more, all offerings of personal favourites from my circle of refugee friends. A woman from Morocco, put on "Missing You" from Biggie Feat 2Pac, and "One Love" from Bob Marly, followed by Viguen, called "king of Iranian Pop" or the "Sultan of Persian Jazz!" Niloofar offered us "Chera Nemiraghsi" meaning "Why Don't You Dance." The mood was celebratory and joyful, and my friends really made my day by the goodbye party they threw for me.

"Thank you, guys. You were all very kind to me. I had really enjoyed this time with you. Thank you for your company, the beer, the delicious cakes, and all your beautiful music. Well done. I appreciate it all, deeply"

I gave them each a big hug and then departed.

It was late, about 11:00 pm, so I went to bed at once. I knew that in the morning I was going to begin a new stage in my life. Undoubtedly, I was entering another promising phase of my journey towards a future that was now somewhat less vague. I was excited to know what destiny would have in store for me.

Before leaving the kitchen, I opened the cupboard, and the fridge to see what I had, as a final check. First, I removed all the stuff I had in the kitchen. I cleaned the cupboard and took only the spices, and fruit into my room to pack, leaving everything else, such as rice, potatoes, sugar, and salt in the kitchen for others to use.

In the yard next to security, a group of asylum seekers with their luggage were waiting for the van to come. Their names were also on the list for dispersal. My friends were also there, gathered around to bid me farewell. As part of our custom, we took pictures and selfies as a remembrance. Then I went into the security office to find Catherine, where I expressed my gratitude for the hard work, kindness, and contribution she had made.

CHAPTER 16

Two vans came and took us to two different directions. The driver of each van informed us where we were going. Three people were going to Middlesbrough, four to Nottingham and two to Newcastle. My last destination was Middlesbrough. We were told that we should stay in our new address until the Home Office contacts us, to call us in for another interview. It would be then that they would decide our respective cases, according to documents and reports we had given them.

At 3 pm, the driver stopped in front of a house in Hope Street, and then we left the van and went inside. The door opened into a doorway.

"Your room is on second floor. It is number three." He spoke to me without looking at me, as he was checking his papers. He then asked me to sign.

"Ok. Sure."

"My number is in the papers, in case there is a problem." He then left in haste.

The front entrance of the house opened into an entryway which could accommodate only a bike or some other small object. On the left side of the entryway, there was a small room where an elderly man from Afghanistan lived. Adjacent to his room, rose a staircase which led to two rooms upstairs. A tiny sitting room with little light was furnished with a dirty two-person sofa, a broken coffee table and a worn-out rug. The kitchen with appliances such as fridge, stove and washing machine was opposite to the entrance. There were two rooms upstairs, one of which, on the right, was mine. The other room was left empty. The house was located a few minutes from a park. It had easy access to a Lidle for shopping as well as a convenient bus station.

When I opened the door, I was deeply shocked by what I saw.

"Gee!" What a mess!" I groaned to myself.

The room was in an absolute shambles. I stood motionless, staring in fright at the stained carpet, the old and torn curtains, the broken drawers, the dirty sofa, and the discoloured wardrobe. The room gave off a terrible stench. The light was extremely poor. Tears began to stream down my face, and I suddenly felt faint. It took me more than half an hour to pull myself together, to take stock of the situation, and decide what I should do-and could -do.

First, I decided to call the van driver who brought me there. I scanned the papers to find the driver's number. I found out that the driver worked for an organisation which provided many different services to customers such as asylum accommodation.

"Hi. I'm Cyrus. You just took me to Hope St. No 40." I said desperately.

"Hi. How can I help you?" he asked.

"I don't like the room. It's dirt. Disgustingly dirty. Can you talk with your manager to change my room?" I begged him for help.

"I'm afraid we can't do that. You will just have to clean the room yourself."

"But some of my friends have been given clean and tidy rooms."

"I know that. Unfortunately, there are only a limited number of rooms available in Middlesbrough. So, it's impossible to change your room for another. If, however, something goes wrong with appliances, let the organisation know, and they will fix them for you."

"Oh." I responded, really disheartened. "Okay, then. Thank you for trying."

I went downstairs to see who else lived in this house. There I saw a well-dressed, elderly man in the sitting room.

The driver had told me on the way that there was another guy from Afghanistan who lived in the house.

"Hello Sir," I said, offering a hopeful smile. At first glance, I could tell that I would like him. I introduced myself to him, and him his name.

"I'm Abdul Azim. You can call me Abdul."

He looked to me like Anthony Quinn, a Mexican American actor. He was a gentle, bearded man in his mid-seventies, wearing a white t-shirt and black shorts. He went to the kitchen and brought me a glass of tea.

"When did you come to the UK?" I asked.

"Twelve years ago."

"So, you have UK citizenship now."

"Unfortunately, I'm still an asylum seeker. I haven't been invited to Home Office Interview yet."

"Why? What's the problem?"

"I have no idea. I call my lawyer every week to see if I can get some good news from Home Office. But each time they only advise me to continue waiting. I'm sick. I have diabetes. I need to move to my own house, but without a positive reply from Home Office that is just not possible," he sighed.

"I should go shopping. I need to buy some detergents to clean up my room," I said.

Lidle was not very far away, so I went on foot. There was a variety of detergents. I bought Dettol, Astonish Flash, Carex Handwash, and Ace for Whites. I came straight home since it was getting dark. There was much work to do, and so I needed to start straight away to deal with the mess.

I put on the gloves and mask that I had bought the day before I left Derby. Now, fully prepared and fully equipped, I set off like a soldier to protect myself and my environment from the dirt and filth that was threatening my health.

Where to start? To make sense of the chaos, I first threw away all the broken and unwanted furniture, like the sofa, carpet, mirror, and chest of drawers. There were also a number of personal items to toss that belonged to the previous occupant, such as clothes, a comb, a hairbrush, and sunglasses. In the drawers I also found things that were for ladies: cosmetics, Always Ultra, tights, and some other women's stuff.

I was repulsed by the sight of all these things and nauseated by the foul smell coming from them. I learned from Abdul Azim, my housemate, that the previous occupant had been bringing street girls home every night. The thought of it made my hair curl.

At 10:30 pm I began the next step, which was hoovering the room. I did it twice to ensure there were no particles of dust, dirt or any food crumbs left. The last step was the use of detergents and surface cleaners. I mixed everything I had and made a bucket of some liquid that was going to eradicate any sorts of microbes, germs, or viruses. I washed everything I could find in the room, even the walls, using the concoction I had made. When I finally finished the cleaning, it was 1:00 in the morning.

I went downstairs to see what I can eat because I was starving to death. Abdul was waiting for me in the living room.

"Please be seated Cyrus. I'm sure you're very hungry."

"Absolutely!" I spoke with a low voice.

He went to the kitchen and started talking in Persian with me.

"I'm thankful to God that they brought you here to this house. Before you came, another guy had lived upstairs. He was a nasty, disrespectful, young boy. He worked very hard but wasted all his money and time on street girls and with rough friends. I really couldn't rest and sleep due to the loud noises that came from his room. He didn't care how old and sick I was." Then Abdul went to the kitchen. "One night I heard him groaning and grumbling for hours. When I went upstairs and knocked on the door to see what the matter was with him, he opened the door, and I was shocked to see the state he was in. All his skin was covered in warts. I felt very sorry for him," he added.

Abdul presented to me a tray containing Khoresht-e Bamieh (Okra stew) and rice. Khoresh Bamieh is a tasty classic Iranian dish of meat, usually lamb, which is stewed with tomatoes, okra, and spices. Khoresh Bamieh comes originally from Khuzestan province in Southern Iran where it is traditionally prepared with tamarined sauce. This stew is also common in many Middle East regions. Okra is oddly known as "Lady's Fingers in the UK."

"The food was very delicious. I'm very grateful for your generosity and hospitality."

"Noush Jaan," he responded back in Farsi. While this can be translated as "Bon Appetit," it is not said to someone before they start eating a meal to tell them "I hope you enjoy your food." Instead, the

Farsi phrase "Noush jaan" or "Nosh joon" is used after someone has finished his meal.

After dinner Abdul went to the kitchen to fetch tea and a plate of biscuits.

"What became of the guy who lived upstairs before me?" I asked.

"I advised him to see a doctor and he did so," Abdul said, "He became better. But I warned him to give up sleeping with prostitutes or he'd risk his health."

As I was exhausted by the clean-up, I asked him for permission to go upstairs to hit the hay.

CHAPTER 17

The next day, I woke up by the pleasing sound of seagulls. Seagulls always give me a sense of freedom. In some traditions, the gull is a wise grandmother who uses her cunning to protect the helpless. They have the ability to sense storms and danger. The words cunning, perseverance, fearlessness, survival, and freedom are symbolically associated with seagull.

After breakfast, I went to find my GP practice to register my name. It was located near Middlesbrough bus station and Aldi. On my way back home, I bought aubergine, tomato, onion, and meat from Aldi and then called Abdul to invite him for lunch as a gratitude for the last night Okra stew. I intended to make Khoresht Bademjoon or Aubergine stew with rice.

After lunch I went to Middlesbrough library to register my name. It was a large library with lots of computers for members to use. I used to go there three times a week to practice theory test because I needed to get the Driver's License, but it was not possible without the interview's positive reply.

On the third day of my arrival in Middlesbrough, I received an Aspen card. It came by post. It was a debit payment card given to UK asylum seekers by the Home Office. The card provided basic subsistence support. £35.00 was deposited into my Aspen card every week.

When things settled down, Jonathan advised me to see Ryan, an honorary curate, from St Botolph Church in Middlesbrough. He then emailed me the church details — email address, contact numbers, and post code.

On 17 June 2018, I decided to go to St Botolph church, so I first googled the Church and found it close to my home address. I set off for the church at about 11 in the morning.

It was a beautiful day with a deep blue sky and a warm gentle breeze that softly rustled the leaves in the trees. Birds chirped expressively from the tree branches. A little dog on a leash behind its owner began to dance, as if it was joining the birds in some natural symphony. The scene produced a beautiful picture of nature. I had no doubt that any passer-by would be filled with joy from so much beauty.

The church came into sight from afar, as I drew closer. The terracotta stone used for the church was inspired, making it look full of life, in comparison to the small, grey houses surrounding it. Its immense proportions drew your gaze to it, commanding attention.

The main entrance to the church was from the front side. After I passed through the portal, I was met by two kind and smiling ladies in the narthex of the church, welcoming people who were attending the service. They were lovely, and introduced themselves to me, sensing I was a newcomer. I eagerly told them who I was, and that I was pleased to be there.

"Welcome to our church." One of the ladies, called Val, said with a big smile.

"Let me introduce you to Grace, Cyrus."

The other lady grasped my hand gently and took me to Grace.

"Grace, this lovely boy has just come to our church." Charlotte said with great enthusiasm.

Grace pointed me towards a table in the corner.

She was a wonderful lady, kind-hearted, and caring. She was a retired headteacher and had been a member of St Botolph church in Middlesbrough for about four decades. We had a brief chat since the church service was about to start.

"Welcome to St Botolph church, Cyrus. Let's now attend the service, and afterwards we can talk," she said gently, laying her hand on my shoulder with a kind smile.

I followed Grace into the church and sat down in a chair next to her. A Reader had just begun reading from Holy Scripture. He had chosen a page from Matthew about the baptism of Jesus Christ by John the Baptist which took place at Bethany beyond the Jordan.

The curate Ryan, a very familiar face to the church family, led the Holy Communion or Eucharist.

The Holy communion was the ritual commemoration of Jesus Last Supper with his disciples, giving them bread and wine during a Passover meal. He commanded them to "do this in memory of me" while referring to the bread as "my body" and the cup of wine as "the blood of my covenant which is poured out for many." This was the central act of Christian worship and was practiced by most Christian churches.

Then we stood in line to receive the sacrament. During this service we had a couple of psalms, sacred songs used in worship, and there was also music.

Before the communion, when the curate said, "The peace of the Lord be always with you," it was one of the loveliest parts of the service since we hugged each other with a smile or touched each other's shoulders and said, "and also with you."

After the service, Grace introduced me to some of the church members present at the narthex. The narthex was a lobby area between the church and the porch. There was a kitchenette there for serving coffee or tea, and biscuits.

Before leaving the church, Grace recommended that I help them with Welcome Break at church. "We serve coffee, tea, and biscuits, and there is a chance to chat and be listened to. It is free of charge for the lonely, vulnerable, and elderly in our area," she said, "and it's useful for you to improve your English and learn how to socialise and mix with people."

CHAPTER 18

That evening I called my mother.

"Hi Mom. How's dad?" I asked.

"He's doing well," she replied. But I felt a quiver of fear or anxiety in her voice. She was hiding something from me. There was sort of sorrow in her tone.

"Is he able to talk now?"

"Ok, give me a minute."

"Hi Cyrus," my father said in a low voice.

"Fine. Miss you dad."

"Me too. How're you getting along?" He looked tired and weak.

"I'm doing well, thank you. How's your leg?"

"As usual."

My father's right leg had had an ulcer before I fled the country. The ulcer was causing severe damage to tissues and bone. His doctor believed that a good diet and plenty of exercise could help control his diabetes, but he found exercise difficult due to his weak body and persistent pain in his leg. Eventually they realised his leg had become infected.

I called my brother the next day to see what the matter with dad was. I was sure that something was wrong.

"Mom doesn't want to disturb you. You're far from us and not able to do anything," he said.

"What's wrong with dad?"

"To be honest, dad is at risk of an amputation due to infection, caused by high blood sugar level and lack of movement."

"If need be, take him to another specialist to see him."

"Ok certainly."

Welcome Break was held at 10 in the morning. Grace was there when I arrived. She introduced me to several of men and women who were going to give a hand. We were a group of seven to ten people.

"Let's pray first, guys. Gather please," Grace said with a big smile. We made a circle. Then each prayed.

Gill prayed that her friend would recover from cancer.

Mary prayed for peace for everyone.

Sarah prayed the war in Yemen would end soon.

I prayed my father would recover.

Susan prayed for the elderly, sick and vulnerable.

Grace prayed to God for help to take the hand of those in need.

Jean prayed that the wars would end in Syria.

After the prayers, we started Welcome Break. I saw very lovely guys coming inside. Most of them were vulnerable or old. They came with their caregivers. They seemed pleased by the blessed moments St Botolph church had created for them. It was an honour for me to serve such fantastic people.

Some of us made coffee or tea. Others made cheese or fruit scones. The rest served the guests. Sometimes we all changed places. At the start I chose to be a server, since that provided me with a better opportunity to chat with people. One of our guests was Richard, a tall and good-looking man, in his early seventies, with long grey hair. He would come with his caregiver because he couldn't perform his daily activities by himself. He talked with great difficulty. I quickly learned to listen more than talk, as many of the people there needed someone to offer a sympathetic ear.

"How did you earn your living before your retirement, Richard?"

"I managed to make a living, being both a singer and a writer," he offered quietly.

"Oh, really? Fabulous!"

"It is true. Show him all the reviews, Richard," suggested his caregiver, proudly.

I was impressed by the gift or aptitude he displayed of himself in writing. He showed me a newspaper extract containing two pieces of poetry with a picture of him. He then asked me to read up the poems for him.

There was a look of contentment on his face, I thought.

"Can I have another white coffee and a cheese scone?"

"Sure Richard."

Richard also told me that he had been a musician and played in a band.

"Next Monday I'll bring a couple of photos of myself with the band."

I had another order from Steve. He was a short, fat guy about 55 years old. He told me that he was keen on cycling and then showed me a picture of him on a bike.

"Do you still cycle Steve?"

"Yeah, only on Tuesdays for an hour." He spoke in the Yorkshire dialect.

The Yorkshire dialect, also Yorkshire English or Yorkie was a dialect spoken in the Yorkshire region of Northern England. The dialect was represented in classic works of literature such as Wuthering Heights written by Emily Bronte and Nicholas Nickleby by Charles Dickens.

"By yourself or in a group?" I asked.

"In a group but accompanied by our caregivers."

"Fabulous Steve. I am also interested in cycling."

I went to the kitchenette to see if the ladies needed a hand. They were over 60 years old but very keen and energetic.

"Will you help me with the scones, Cyrus," Emily said. "How's your room?"

While preparing the scones, I told her that my room was in a terrible mess.

"Do you need help with the clean up?"

"It's really kind of you to say that. I've already tidied it up. It took me three days to finish it," I said with a smile.

"Do you need anything to furnish your room with?" She asked, "for example, a table and chairs, or a carpet."

"I need a table and two chairs, but I don't want to inconvenience any friends for that."

"Ok I'll sort it out for you. Don't worry."

We finished the Welcome Break work at 12:00. Then in half an hour we cleaned up the church hall. I was just about to leave when Grace approached.

"I want to thank you for your hardworking and kindness today, Cyrus."

"Don't mention it," I said. "I had a fabulous time today."

"Your help was invaluable and very helpful. To be honest, we were over the moon watching you socialising with the vulnerable and treating them equally, politely, respectfully and patiently."

While cooking for lunch, I had a call from my lawyer.

She reassured me that the errors on my details had been corrected and sent to the Home Office. There were serious mistakes in the report made by the immigration officer at the airport.

In the evening, I heard a loud knock at the door. She was Grace and her husband Ryan.

"We thought you might need carpet," she said. "We're always on hand to help you so please just let us know"

"I really appreciate your kindness."

I was amazed to see such respectful people, giving me a hand.

"How's your father?" Ryan asked.

"He's in a critical condition. He's going to be taken to hospital for some treatment."

"God bless him. We'll pray for him to recover soon."

CHAPTER 19

A few weeks passed without hearing anything from Home Office, so I became alarmed since several of my friends from hostel were invited for interview.

I called my lawyer. She advised me to wait until I receive a letter from Home Office.

"Many people are waiting for months, some even two years or more for their interview. This is frustrating. But you should make use of the time to get ready for the interview."

Her words persuaded me to evade the issue and instead to work on my case. *It was futile to eat myself,* I thought.

Interview was the last episode or stage in the life of an asylum seeker. Each had to answer in detail the reasons for claiming asylum. The interview might last several hours from two to six hours and lots of questions needed be answered. Preparation for this interview was very important so one had to know what questions might come and how they looked like.

One Sunday after the service, as I was having coffee with Grace, Emily and her husband, Jack, approached.

"Hi Cyrus. I have a table and two chairs for you. If you're at home this afternoon, we'll carry them to you."

One day in early July, I had a call from GP surgery. They arranged an appointment with me for a blood test and respiratory system check as routine checks carried out for all asylum seekers and refugees.

"Are you registered with us?"
"Yes, I am. I guess in June."
"Can I see the Home Office document or paper?"
"Here you are."
"Lovely, have a seat in the lobby please."

CHAPTER 20

It was about 4 pm. I had a call from Emily to check if I were at home. I went to the kitchen to prepare coffee and tea. I had some cake that I had made the night before. I was very happy that Emily and her husband, Jack, were coming.

At 4:30 pm they showed up, apologising for being late.

Jack and I carried the table and chairs upstairs and Emily came with a vase of white lilies.

"Lovely flowers, Emily. Thank you so much."

"Happy you like it. It's good to have flowers around you," she said with a big smile.

I enjoyed their company. They were very kind.

"What was your profession in Iran, Cyrus?" Jack asked.

"Primary school teacher."

"Fabulous! Your English is perfect."

"Thank you, Jack. You know, I have a degree in English Language and literature," I said. "Your name reminds me of an American novelist and poet. Can you guess his name? He was best known for the novel 'On the Road.'"

"I have no idea, Cyrus. I'm interested only in science. But Emily is fond of literature. I'm sure she can tell you the name." He looked surprised by the question.

"I'm not sure about the author's name but I've heard about this work." Emily said with a laughter.

"What is his name any way?"

"Jack Kerouac," I said. "He pioneered the Beat Generation."

"Emily loves poetry. Sometimes she writes poems."

"Marvellous! I'm fond of poetry too."

"Cyrus tell me a poet whose first name is Emily." Emily had a playful expression on her face.

"You're inviting me for a challenge?" I burst out laughing.

"I want to avenge my husband's defeat and mine of course."

"Ok. Let me see. First name Emily! Aha! Here we go! Emily Dickenson."

"Well done. I love her poetry, especially 'Because I Could Not Stop for Death.'"

"I've read it. It's beautiful. The main theme of this poem is death and immortality. It's an exploration of both the inevitability of death and the uncertainty of the afterlife," I said. "I've also read 'I Heard a Fly Buzz—When I Died,' my favourite poem."

"Wonderful! You're very good at literature."

"There is another author, your namesake. She wrote 'Wuthering Heights.' It's a very sad story."

"Emily Bronte!" she said. "I don't like it. It's dark. It's about revenge, demonic, and passion."

"I've read it too. I agree. It's so depressing. It should be the product of her environment, and this has directly influenced her writing."

"She had no close friends during her life maybe because she was interested in mysticism and a life of solitude," she said.

A great sense of belonging was beginning to shape, a feeling of belonging to a family. I had not felt it until I entered St Botolph church and started working at Welcome Break as a volunteer. Something was growing inside me. I could feel a glimmer of hope was touching me. It seemed that life was finally showing its good side. Light was soothing my heavy heart.

"Cyrus, we really enjoyed your company and the chat. Please let us know if you need something. You can count on us. Just say the word," Jack said.

When I woke up the next day, the sun was streaming through the window. It was 9:15. I went downstairs to take a shower. I saw Abdul in the kitchen, preparing breakfast. He was rather out of sorts.

"You don't look fine Abdul Azim. What's wrong?" I asked.

"Well. I've been poorly since yesterday."

"Got to go to GP. Do you need my company?"

"No thanks. A friend of mine is going to pick me up."

After shower, I had my breakfast in the living room, and then I went up to my room. I noticed I had missed some calls from my brother and Grace.

"Hi Bardia. I just saw your calls."

"Hi Cyrus. Dad is not fine. We took him to Milad Hospital in Tehran."

"What's wrong with dad? You look as though you've been crying."

"As you know because of diabetes and high blood sugar level, his leg has been infected."

"What should we do, Bardia? How can we help him?"

"I talked with a doctor about the infection. He advised me that father must stay in hospital until the infection disappears."

"Does it work?"

"They have no idea."

"I can provide medicines if it is unavailable in the market."

"Let's see. I'll check it with the doctor and call you back. Doctor is here."

Abdul knocked on the door as I was waiting for my brother's call.

"I should be off now. I have prepared lunch for both. You're my guest, so don't cook any. Come downstairs at about three pm if it's ok with you."

"Sure. Thanks. Do you need anything to purchase for you?"

"I've everything, Khoda Hafez." Then he left. Khoda Hafez or Khodafez in Persian is a common parting phrase that is used in Iran and Afghanistan.

I had missed Grace's call, so I called her.

"Hello Grace. How are you? You called me this morning."

"I want to be sure if you like to come for the Welcome Break this Monday."

"Absolutely. I'm very interested. You can count on me Grace."

"I've good news for you."

"What's that?" Tell me please. I can't wait to hear it."

"Do you like to work as an interpreter since you are good at English and fond of interpreting."

"I'm thinking about it. It crossed my mind when I was at GP practice for blood test."

"Fabulous. I'll send you the link. Check it out. It should be useful for you. There is a course you should take. There are lots of asylum seekers coming to the UK, especially to Middlesbrough and other places like Stockton which is near Middlesbrough and Darlington. So, interpreters are needed at GPs, Eye and Dental centres," she said. "See you on Sunday, Cyrus."

I checked the link. There was a course held at a community centre in Stockton-on-Tees. It was a four-months course starting in September. So, I had enough time to apply for the course.

I called Bardia to see what was going on. He was supposed to talk to a doctor. Honestly, I didn't have the guts to hear any bad news. I missed my family and was worried about my father's health.

"His medicines are available at the pharmacies, but they should first see the result of the MRIs and scans, and then decide what they can do."

I was unable to sleep. I was alarmed to find out how terrible his condition was.

"Can I see him once more?" I wondered what would happen to father.

Abdul came back from GP practice at around 2 pm. He was in the kitchen when I went down into the sitting room.

"Hi Cyrus. Lunch will be served in a minute."

"What have you cooked?"

"Ghormeh Sabzi. I guess you Iranians love this stew," he said smiling at me.

Ghormeh Sabzi is my favourite Iranian food. It is a very popular dish in Iran. The stew is made from several types of herbs such as parsley, cilantro or coriander, spinach, and fenugreek. Other ingredients are kidney beans or red beans, dried limes, and meat, preferably lamb. It is served with rice.

"It's very delicious Abdul. You have a flair for making food."

But there was something peculiar about his cuisine—appetising and mouth-watering, but terribly peppery. There is too much ground red peppers in his dish.

After the lunch, I helped him with doing the dishes.

CHAPTER 21

I woke up early today because it was time to attend the church service and I was really enthusiastic about that.

A large crowd had gathered this time. I saw Grace sitting in the third row on the right. The seat next to her was empty, so I went to sit there. She nodded her head and smiled. The choir was performing the Hallelujah, accompanied by music. Ryan started talking about the nature of baptism.

"Baptism is a sacrament of admission into Christianity. It is performed by sprinkling water on the head or by immersing in water, three times due to Trinity: God the father, God the son and God the Holy Spirit, in other words, one God in three forms. According to the Gospels, John the Baptist baptised Jesus. Matthew portrays the risen Christ, issuing the Great Commission to his followers: Go therefore and make disciples of all nations, baptising them in the name of the Father, of the Son and of the Holy Spirit, teaching them to observe all that I have commanded you." Ryan looked with a smile at the baby who was going to be baptised then continued. "Baptism represents the forgiveness and cleansing from the sin that comes through faith in Jesus Christ."

He then introduced the couple and the baby, and he proceeded.

At the end there was music and songs to celebrate this spiritual and holy event. Parents of the baby had prepared coffee, fruit juice, and lots of finger foods for the attenders.

Grace approached as I was leaving the church.

"Ryan and I would like to invite you for lunch this Wednesday. Can you come?"

"Why not, Grace. I accept it with pleasure."

On Monday morning, as I was having breakfast, I heard a letter drop into a letter box. It was from Home Office. At last it was my interview date —30 August.

I had one month to prepare myself for the interview. I was delighted for the news but worried for the outcome. I informed Grace of the interview at Welcome Break.

"Good news guys! Cyrus is going to have the interview this August," she called out. "Let's gather to pray. The guests are waiting behind the door."

Each prayed but this time I was the centre of attentions.

"I pray for your father to get well and cope with his condition and I pray God to be with you in your interview," Emily said.

"We are sorry to know your father is so ill. We will pray for him. Also, we will pray for you as you cannot be with him. And we pray that you will pass the interview successfully. May God bless you and keep you in his care," Sylvia said.

"Oh, I am sorry to hear your father is poorly, Cyrus. It sounds like your father is having a tough time at the moment. He is in our prayers. I pray he would recover soon," Elaine said. "I also pray to God that He be with you at the interview."

After the prayers, the door opened, and the guests came into the church hall. We started Welcome Break. We had a pretty hectic day! I was very delighted to see smile on their face. There was real satisfaction in helping these lovely people to overcome their monotony and bringing happy moments in their life. These people enjoyed our reception and the chat with us.

Today we had a birthday party for one of the guests, Meg. Grace asked me to take the cake she had provided to Meg's table. We all shouted, "Happy birthday Meg."

I looked for Richard to have a chat with him, but he was absent. He used to sit at a table next to a bookcase whose book of poems laid there. Part of his book was about man's loneliness in modern society. These poems were written in his early thirties. The other part comprised themes of Man's hope and dream for future.

"Not only does he have a knack for observing real life in his poetry, but he does so in a way that shows tenderness and a great wit," his support worker once said.

On our first conversation, I asked Richard to show me more of his amazing work, and he was happy to do so. He also shared with me with enthusiasm a couple of photos of him in a band carrying a red electric guitar.

The next Monday I noticed Richard's absence once more. I felt worried about him, so I went to Grace who was busy talking with guests.

"Do you have any idea where Richard, the poet, as we used to call him, is?" I asked. "It's for three weeks that I don't see him."

"Let me see who can get in touch with him or his caregiver," she said and left.

After a few minutes she came back, looking so gloomy.

"I'm very sorry to tell you Richard passed away two weeks ago in St James hospital."

"May he rest in God's peace." I felt down after I heard the news. *Welcome Break had lost a regular member!*

I left the church and walked down Walpole Street towards my house. It was depressing to see the sky grow dark at this time of the day

As the interview was approaching, I tried to focus only on my case. Without the approval from Home Office, I was not able to work or use any services such as open an account or get driver's licence. So I had to pass the interview successfully. Grace and Ryan advised me to be baptised before the interview. They designated a date to carry out the task. I was overjoyed by the news—a positive encouragement.

The day before my baptism, Ryan started to acquaint me with the rituals and symbols of baptism, scriptural readings and prayers.

"I'll keep you posted on the latest news. Your baptism will probably be on the first week of August," Ryan said to me on the last day of induction course.

I was thankful and very happy that things were looking up, I felt.

But the joy didn't last. *Nice moments are always transient,* I thought.

Too many thoughts about my father's illness, Home Office interview, and a dim future ahead of me were buzzing in my head but my father's physical health condition dominated the others. I knew there was something seriously wrong with my father. Every day I expected to have a disappointing call. Panic raced through my body. My heart pounded so hard that I could hear the beatings. I was in a bad state of mind. I couldn't really concentrate. During the day I tried to entertain myself with the theory test, ride my bike or prepare myself for the interview. But during the night, I couldn't help making time move. In fact, time stopped. Nightmares, Time's accomplice, triggered by waking me up and I stayed awake until morning.

"Am I able to see him again? What will happen if they amputate his leg? Can he survive it?" I was preoccupied by the questions I couldn't answer.

Next, hives appeared to affect my body, making me stay awake during the night as nightmares did so to me. They were raised, itchy rash. In the morning I called GP practice to consult my doctor.

"They're hives. There can be many causes," doctor said. "In most cases, hives are caused by allergic reaction to a medication or food or a reaction to an irritant in the environment. Sometimes, stress causes the hives."

"They sting and hurt," I said.

"Don't worry. I give you some tablets. Cetirizine Hydrochloride 10 mg will do you good."

CHAPTER 22

When I arrived home, Abdul told me that a new asylum seeker had been brought here. His luggage was in the sitting room. He was supposed to stay in the room opposite mine.

"Where's he from?"

"From Karaj, Iran, I think he said. He's outdoors, doing shopping."

As we were talking, he pushed the door open.

"Hi everyone. Abdul Azim told me you're from Iran," he said.

"Yes, I am. I lived in Tehran." I replied.

"Glad to meet you, what's your name, anyway?"

"Cyrus. And You?"

"Parham."

"Which hostel did you come from, Parham?"

"I come from Birmingham."

"How long have you been there?"

"Nearly thirty-five days."

"How was the hostel like?"

"Frustrating!" he said. "Very crowded. Rooms were small and untidy."

"Ok. I see you are tired. We'll talk later. If you need a hand, please let me know."

"Thanks, Cyrus. By the way, I'm looking for a church. Do you know one?"

"Yes, sure. My church. St Botolph church. I'll take you there on Sunday."

"Thanks a million. Cheers," said Parham with a big smile.

I noticed that he was filled with an overwhelming sense of relief.

Relief flooded through me after the conversation I had with Parham. His company helped lessen some of the pressures I had because of my dad's condition.

Grace called me at around 11 am to double-check with me to see whether I could join them for lunch. I informed her that a new asylum seeker from Iran had arrived and wished to attend St Botolph church.

"Take him with you, Cyrus. We have enough food for four of us. We'll be happy to see him," Grace said.

But Parham couldn't make it since he had an appointment with GP practice.

Ryan and Grace lived in a very beautiful and wealthy area in the west of Middlesbrough. I took a bus and got there within an hour. The house was elegantly furnished. To break the ice, Grace gave me a tour of the house. We started upstairs, where family pictures were hung on all the walls. She proudly explained who was who, and it was a pleasure for me to see everyone in this big, English family for the first time. There were also fine paintings on the wall.

She also took me to Ryan's study, knowing that I was interested in literature. She picked a book from a shelf and gave it to me. It was "The Oxford Book of English Verse," an anthology, ranging from the Thirteenth to the Nineteenth.

"This is a gift for you from Ryan and me. I know you are interested in poetry." The book began with Cuckoo Song written by an anonymous writer.

The walls, in the study, consisted of shelves full of invaluable books, most of which were about theology, the Gospels, priesthood, and several poetry and novels.

"If you are interested in reading, you can borrow any of the books in the study."

I saw 'To the Lighthouse.' It was one of my favourite novels by Virginia Woolf.

"Can I borrow this book?"

"Sure. Do you know what she is famous for?"

I felt she was testing me, just for the fun of it.

"She was best known for her novels, 'Mrs Dalloway' and 'To the Lighthouse.' She was considered a modernist author and a pioneer in the use of Stream of Consciousness as a narrative device. She was also one of the first feminists."

"Well done, Cyrus. I see you have an aptitude for literature."

For lunch she had made Greek Moussaka. This classic dish of layered sliced potato, baked aubergine and minced lamb is topped with creamy bechamel sauce.

While eating, Grace asked me about my dad's physical health condition. We also talked about my new housemate, Parham, and about Home Office interview.

"The following Sunday, we will pray for your father at the church. We will beg the Lord to speed his recovery and get him back on his feet soon," Ryan said.

As to Home Office interview, Grace advised me to get prepared for Baptism. She had already arranged it with church.

"Remember to bring Parham to church."

"Absolutely. Parham can't wait to see you and the church. He is eager to attend our church."

CHAPTER 23

Parham said to me that in Izmir, which had been a hub for refugees and migrants, seeking to illegally cross to Europe, got in touch with smugglers with the help of other refugees. He had paid his life savings to smugglers £2500 each to get them onto an old fishing boat by way of Aegean Sea from Turkey to Europe. Despite the numerous tragedies that occurred to refugees in the Aegean Sea and the camps afterwards in Greece, Parham ended up so lucky.

Parham had bad unpleasant memories about his journey. He was kept with others in dirty houses without much clean water and with very little food. Smugglers treated them badly. They were very abusive and aggressive. In fact, they enjoyed treating refugees the way they did, and it didn't matter to them that they had paid all the money.

While in a camp in Greece, Parham had witnessed a man who asked a couple's young daughter into their tent to play games on his phone. He then zipped up the tent. When the girl came back, she had marks on her arms and neck. Later, the girl described how she was sexually abused.

When I was in Derby, an Iranian asylum seeker disclosed a very horrible story that befell her fourteen-year-old son in Calais. Tears streamed down her face when she struggled to tell me. "Three ruffians or bullies took my son away from me by force. I begged and pleaded with them to keep their hands off my son, but they didn't care or listen. I then shouted seeking for help, but no one dared to interfere."

I came back home at 5 pm. Abdul was in his room, talking aloud on his cell phone. He had left the door ajar. Parham was outdoors shopping maybe. I went upstairs to take a nap after a long walk from Grace's home.

On Sunday, second week of August, I was informed by the church that the time for my baptism had been arranged. Both baptism and confirmation would be on Sunday 18 August at 6 pm. Everyone congratulated me warmly on the new birth that was approaching.

To my amazement, Malcom and Vicky, a fabulous couple, and the church regulars, invited me to lunch at a Fish and Chips restaurant in Whitby, a seaside town in Yorkshire, northern England.

The town was split by the river Esk, on the East cliff, there lay the ruined Gothic Whitby Abbey which was a source of inspiration for Bram Stoker to write 'Dracula'. The captain Cook memorial Museum was also worth visiting since it was the house where Cook once lived. James Cook was a British explorer, navigator and captain in the British Royal Navy.

It was my first time to have this English Fish and Chips dish. The reason for the invitation was just to make me happy before my baptism.

They lived near Linthorpe Cemetery, which was a large, beautiful, forested area in central Middlesbrough. Linthorpe cemetery was one of Middlesbrough's oldest graveyards, where the earliest burials dated back to 1869. I used to ride my bicycle through the cemetery and see the old graves every now and then. *It gave me sort of a sense of comfort and hope to continue,* I felt.

CHAPTER 24

One of the best and most significant moments of my life was my baptism which took place at our church on 18 August. At 6 pm about ninety people gathered to witness my baptism, most of whom were friends and families from St Botolph church and Welcome Break. Each came with a gift and card to celebrate and share their joy with me. The church also provided a cake with my name on it and food to be served after the ceremony.

I was baptised and confirmed by Fr Stephen, a bishop from another church, and during which I gave a short testimony to my faith.

After the ceremony, Ryan gave a talk on the nature of baptism.

"According to the Bible, the first known baptism occurred with Jesus Christ when he was baptised in the River Jordan by his disciple John, known as John the Baptist. This was a major event in the life of Jesus which was described in three of the Gospels: Matthew, Mark, and Luke. It took place at Al-Maghtas or Bethany Beyond Jordan." Ryan then read a chapter from Matthew 3:11. The verse was related to the teachings of John the Baptist. John predicted that he would be followed by someone much greater than himself.

"I indeed baptise you with water unto repentance, but He that cometh after me is mightier than I, whose shoes I am not worthy to bear. He shall baptise you with the Holy Ghost and with fire."

Baptism can take place in various locations—in the church, at a lake, or at the ocean, in a stream, in bathtubs, or pond. I myself was submerged in submersion pool borrowed from another church. After the submersion, I changed my clothes since I was dripping wet. I had been advised to take some clothes with me.

As I entered the narthex, the attenders and guests started cheering, with one voice "Congratulations, Cyrus!"

"Happy New Birth!" Grace cheered.

"Warmest wishes on your baptism and welcome to our community of faith," Chris said, smiling at me.

I received big, warm hugs, gifts and cards. I stood at the table, in the centre with Grace, Emily, Parham, the Bishop, and some others, on both sides. We took photos and selfies with each other.

There was a big chocolate cake decorated with strawberries and cream on the table. My name was written on the cake. There were also a wide variety of finger foods such as chicken tenders, finger chips, fish stakes, ham and cheese roll-ups, and mini quiche spread out on the table. All provided by friends and church regular attenders. There was also coffee and biscuits at the kitchenette.

It was, in fact, one of the most exciting and memorable moments of my life, I thought.

The day after my baptism, I went to Middlesbrough library to practice theory test for preparing myself for the Driver's Licence. I liked the library. I felt comfortable there as I didn't have anything else to do of course. I used to go there twice or three times a week. I was planning to get the Driver's Licence as I was advised for any future activities, but first I had to pass the Home Office interview. Positive result was prerequisite to any future activities such as studying at college, opening an account, or getting the Driver's Licence.

At the church, John, one of the church attenders approached and asked me to see if I needed a bicycle in response to my request to Grace. I had asked her to help me with a bicycle since I wanted it to go to the library, GP practice or to hang around in Middlesbrough. John told me that he had a friend in the Centre who could provide me with a bicycle until I buy one myself.

Everyday Parham and I cycled for a few hours along River Tees. We started from Newport Bridge. We had to use the metal staircase to carry our bicycles down the bridge towards the riverside path. We sometimes walked along the river from the barrage to the Newport bridge through the nature reserve. During the night the bridge was beautifully lit. Tees Newport Bridge in Middlesbrough was a vertical-lift bridge and one of the oldest in the UK, linking Middlesbrough with Stockton-on-Tees. It was three miles west of Middlesbrough.

We cycled from one side of the River Tees towards Stockton, then back to Middlesbrough from the other side. It was our daily routine. It was a cathartic experience — trying to forget our troubles and think of a better life and a promising future ahead.

We used to stop at the "Framing Teesdale Way" close to Tees Newport Bridge to rest and take photos and selfies. It was a metal frame and a small bench or seat for cyclists or walkers who pass by, to go into the frame and take fabulous photos in a landscape with the River Tees on the right and Tees Newport Bridge in a distance in front.

CHAPTER 25

Around 11:00 in the morning I received a call as I was on the way to Middlesbrough library. It was my brother, Bardia. His news was terrible and disappointing.

"Doctors need our permission to amputate dad's right leg," he said despondingly. "His leg is severely infected."

"What happens if we refuse?" I said. *He is not healthy and strong enough to bear the surgery*, I thought.

"His doctor told me that the tissues in the leg have died due to poor circulation. Without adequate blood flow, the body's cells cannot get oxygen and nutrients they need from blood stream. As a result, the tissue begins to die and gets infected."

"Medication doesn't help?" I asked.

"Unfortunately, his condition is very bad. Infection can spread through the body soon," he said. "Doctors tried medication, but it didn't work."

"What portion of the leg is going to be removed?"

"I'm sorry to say, it is unfortunately above the knee." Bardia wept as he was talking.

"Can father make the decision?" I asked.

"He was given a choice between preserving the limb that surely could not be fully restored and amputation. But he is not in good condition to decide. He is unconscious most of the time."

"What does mom say? Does she agree?"

My mother believed that father was not healthy enough to go through another surgery again. She can't really make a decision over my dad's condition. This had placed mom in a serious dilemma because both paths go to nowhere, or neither option seem very desirable.

My father had had a surgery several years ago. The main reason was also the infection of the bladder that resulted in inflammation. This caused intense pain and changes in urination. He was unable to empty his bladders. A urologist prescribed him with antibiotics and anti-inflammatory medications to relieve his pain and inflammation, but the medication didn't help. One night, I heard him howling in pain.

"I can't urinate," he cried out.

My mother and I took father to a hospital. They inserted a catheter or a small tube into the urethra so that urine could be drained into a collection bag. A night shift doctor advised us to take dad to a specialist for a check-up since the scrotum had grown in size, sort of swollen, and dark red in colour. In two weeks, the scrotum became darker, bigger, and smelly.

My father was hospitalised for two months due to the infection of the scrotum. Unfortunately, high blood sugar levels weakened my dad's immune system defence, along with the reduction in blood flow, resulted in the rise of infection and finally damaging the scrotum.

The role of the Infectious Disease doctor was very important in controlling the infection of the scrotum. The doctor used to come to the hospital twice a week to check up my father's condition and to give him new prescription and medication. Unluckily, some nurses didn't do their duty properly so my brother and I, in turn, washed father's broken scrotum with soap or shampoo under doctor's supervision twice a day. After two months father's scrotum was treated. There was no infection anymore. The hospital discharged my father and referred him to his urologist. After seeing father's scrotum, and the scans and MRIs, doctor smiled and showed his two thumbs up, then said that our efforts were fruitful and successful. By this news, we all breathed a sigh of relief. We called mom to tell her that dad survived danger in the end. We felt nothing but relief when it was over.

"Now that there is no symptom of infection, I will do my turn by a reconstructive surgery," doctor said.

After five days in hospital, my father recovered, and smile returned to his face.

Prostate problem and open-heart surgery had weakened my dad. He was no longer healthy enough to bear another surgery.

The amputation of leg was finally decided by my mom since dad was not in good state of mind to choose. Meanwhile, his doctor told Bardia that the infection was about to spread all his body and it would endanger father's health condition.

CHAPTER 26

In the evening, after my telephone conversation with Bardia, I took the bicycle to the Riverside Tees. I just wanted to be alone. The sky was filled with dark clouds and was about to rain. I carried the bicycle down the metal stairs and then took the path towards Tees Barrage Bridge. Cycling along the River Tees was more than just a hobby or amusement. It was a sort of escape or forgetting for me when things weren't going well. But this time it was of no use. Nothing could prevent me from thinking of my dad. It had become an obsession. Dad was everywhere. I sometimes had strange dreams about my dad. He appeared for a short time. I asked him to stay with me. One night my father and I were in some sort of forest. The sun was setting. Everywhere was dark. I saw him in the middle of forest standing by a huge tree. Dad said to me that he should go but at first, he should deal with an important job.

"I have a duty to accomplish first."

"What is it, father?" I asked. He looked worried and in a hurry.

"Take care of your mother and tell her not to weep for me."

"Why you say that." I begged him to stay. "Let's go home dad."

"I can't. It's time to go now," he said. "Remember to stay with your mom and look after her."

I woke up. It was 3:00 am. I couldn't sleep. I made coffee and tried to think of what dad had told me. In the morning I called mom to tell her what I saw in my dream.

"Don't worry Cyrus. He'll be fine. Things will look up!" she said.

On my way back to the Newport Bridge where I started cycling, I entered a bar to have a glass of Corona-Extra. The place had great views to the Riverside Tees. There was a caravan site right behind the bar, so it was very handy for anyone staying there. It had a pleasant atmosphere with fantastic menu, exceptional service, and friendly and polite staff.

It was devastating for someone like me, far from home, to see one's dear undergo such a surgery.

The following day my father's leg was amputated. He was kept in ICU because he needed close monitoring and critical care to recover.

"Does father know about the amputation?"

He was not in good state of health and most of the time he was sleepy or giddy, sometimes unconscious. We were also under pressure from the hospital. We were told several times that infection is being spread all through his body and probably might infect other patients.

"We can't keep him here," his doctor said. So a prompt decision must be made.

"Take him home if you are not happy or disagree with the amputation," he added.

We accepted the surgery because we thought he could at least survive.

CHAPTER 27

On 30 August 2018, at 11:30, the interview was held in Newcastle. Grace had arranged it with Sean and Juliet, a middle-aged couple, to take me to Newcastle. They came to our church regularly.

They picked me at 8:30 from my house, 40 Hope Street. We arrived on the spot at 10:15. As we had enough time, they took me to Starbucks to have coffee. Sean and Juliet noticed that I was having stress, so they encouraged me to stay cool.

Before I leave the car, Juliet started praying for me.

"All-powerful God, I pray that you would give Cyrus success in his interview. Give him confidence Lord, to speak clearly and to answer the questions with wisdom. You are with him. You never leave his side."

"We'll be here to pick you up," Sean said.

It was 11:15 pm. I entered the Home Office building.

I left the building at 2:30 pm. The interview lasted for three hours including a 15-minutes break. Home Office provided an interpreter for me. The interviewer after introducing herself, asked me first if I was happy with the interpreter and her interpretation, if I needed a break and if I was ready for the interview.

The questions were divided into six categories:

1. About you such as your birthday, nationality, and if you have been convicted of a criminal offence.
2. About your journey such as when you left your country, if you travelled through other countries on your way to the UK.

3. Why are you claiming asylum? There were questions like why can't you return to your country? What could happen to you if you did? Has the threat affected other people? Are you in contact with your family?
4. Questions about Christianity: to see if you are really interested in Christianity.
5. Questions about Islam: to see if you had truly been a Muslim.
6. About your country: to prove you are from Iran.

Outside the building Juliet and Sean were waiting for me.

"How did your interview go?" Juliet asked.

"Everything went well except my escape from the plain-clothes police at the house church. The interviewer didn't accept it at first but after I explained three times she agreed. She told me that she couldn't believe a word of how I had made the escape with the presence of plain-clothes police.

"Don't worry Cyrus. You'll pass it. At the time of the interview, Juliet and I were praying for you. Our friends who had gathered at Botolph church were also praying for you."

"I'm deeply grateful to all those who took the trouble to go to church to pray for me. I also do appreciate your help, your company, and your time."

"Absolutely."

On the way back to Middlesbrough, Grace called me to see how things were going. She was worried about my interview. That's why she went to church early in the morning with other ladies to pray for me. She treated me like her own son. It was amazing to see how responsible Grace was feeling of me and others.

Sean pulled the car over at a restaurant near Sunderland docks in Sunderland. The restaurant had a beautiful view of the North Sea, and it was a warm, sunny day. Dozens of seabirds surrounded the area. They varied in size and in species, among them I could see gulls, tern, and guillemot. Some were in the air, flying and diving. Some were on the shore, hopping around or walking. They seemed to be endlessly trying to find something to eat. Sean chose a table outside the restaurant. There was a gentle breeze that carried the shrills of the birds.

CHAPTER 28

I remember, it was 9 August, in the evening, I had a call from Grace. She invited me to lunch outdoors. She sent me a message with the restaurant details. "We'll pick you at 1:30 in the afternoon."

I googled the restaurant. It was close to the church and not far from Hope Street where I lived. I called her back to say I'll make it myself to the restaurant.

I was at Kleez Restaurant the day after. Grace was sitting at a table with Ryan, and Parham, my housemate. I was very surprised to see a waitress come with a cake.

"Surprise!" Ryan shouted with joy, and then, a great cheer went up from the table.

"Happy Birthday Cyrus." Parham spoke joyfully and began to dance in an Iranian style. He was the centre of attention, and other customers began to applaud.

It was my 55th birthday and Ryan and Grace thoughtfully presented me with a gift-wrapped book. It was "The Nation's Favourite Poems," as they knew that I was very interested in literature. Parham was also generous to me, gifting a black Cross bike helmet.

I chose chicken Parmesan with homemade fries and salad. It was very delicious.

After lunch Grace ordered ice cream and we all enjoyed it with birthday cake and coffee. She then requested that I should choose a poem from the book to read for them. I opened the book and chose

"Stopping by Woods on a Snowy Evening" by Robert Frost. It was one of my favourite poems, especially these lines:

> The woods are lovely, dark and deep,
> But I have promises to keep,
> And miles to go before I sleep,
> And miles to go before I sleep.

The following day in the morning, as I was going to the library to practice theory test, a poster stuck to the wall drew my attention. It was advertising the Status Quo, an English rock band. As a teenager I used to listen to Status Quo. It was one of my favourite bands. It was a thrill to see but also a surprise to note that the lead singer had somehow become old and lost his hair.

From the money I had saved, I purchased the ticket. The band was playing live at Middlesbrough Town Hall, located right in the heart of the town centre. It was my first presence at a concert in the UK, and I was overjoyed.

As I was humming 'In the Army Now,' my mobile rang. It was Bardia, my brother. His voice was low and a bit shaky.

"Dad is not doing well," he said, and then began to weep.

"Why? What has happened?"

"After the amputation, his health worsened. Infection is spreading all throughout his body."

"But his doctor told you that amputation would successfully treat this, didn't he?"

"Yes, absolutely. He had already told us the surgery would be the only option and persisted that it would likely go very well. He is being given the best antibiotic, but unfortunately, the drug doesn't seem to be working in his body. It isn't stopping the infection."

"Did you talk with Dad after surgery?"

"After surgery, he was taken to the ICU. He's still there. Unconscious. We're waiting outside the ICU to see him when he wakes up."

"Who's there with you?"

"Only me. Mom was here yesterday. She's old, you know, and can't stay in the hospital for long. I advised her to go home."

"I'm so sorry that I'm not there with you. I know you're experiencing very difficult moments."

"Yes, it's hard not having someone with me through this. But I know you care, and I appreciate your calls and support."

"By the way, your friend, Armin, was here, he came to see Dad."

We hadn't been in touch after I fled Iran. I thought he might get into trouble if plai- clothes police realised he was contacting me. I didn't want to ruin his life. I missed him so much. We met at least twice a week at school. Armin was from Rasht, a city in the north of Iran, known as the 'city of Rain'. His family moved to Tehran when Armin was a baby. He was around fifteen when his father died in a car accident. We first met at school nearly ten years ago as a colleague. I am thankful that I have such a lovely friend. I didn't really know what would have become of me if Armin hadn't opened his door for me the night I fled from the church house.

"Tell Armin to contact me if it is safe to do so," I said to Bardia.

CHAPTER 29

Two days later, at about six in the morning, my father died in hospital, despite all the efforts made for his survival. It was the saddest and most difficult news for a son to hear, especially alone in a foreign land, far far away. Bardia was at his side when father died. It was very painful for me not to be there for my father in his final days, and it was heartbreaking not to be there for his funeral. I felt so very sorry that Bardia had to face all of that alone. At least for the funeral there were relatives and friends who could step in to help and advise. But I should have been there to help with arrangements for the funeral.

I called my mother and Bardia several times to grieve with them, but I couldn't ever reach them. After the news of my father's death spread, we received many calls and messages from people who knew us. They all wanted to express their sympathies and condolences for the death of my father.

My mother eventually called me and indicated that she was very busy with the calls.

"I want to come home, mom. I'm not ok. I can't stay here. I'm going to be at dad's funeral."

"No please! They will put you in prison as soon as you arrive at the airport. Don't do it," she said, "Your coming back won't bring back your father, will it? This will hurt us, all of us. And mostly you. Your father's soul will become restless and sad if you get into trouble. Bardia and I need you. Let me tell you something to open your eyes. Do you remember Siamak, Fataneh's son?"

"Oh, yes! Our previous neighbour in Iran, what has happened to him?"

"I saw Fataneh at a market yesterday. She was very upset. When I asked her what the problem was, she told me that her son was in prison."

"But Siamak lives in Germany."

"Yes, it's true. But when he came back to visit his parents, plain-clothes police arrested him at the airport."

"Why mom?"

"They had found out that Siamak had converted to Christianity."

"I am so very sorry to hear that, mom."

"Please don't come. If they arrest you, we'll all face ruin. Your father has died. Yes? But do you want to see my destruction too?"

"Ok mom. You are right. Calm down. I won't come."

"Promise Kourosh?"

"I promise mom!"

"I'll get someone to contact you, to set it up so that you can watch your dad's burial on WhatsApp."

"Good. Thanks mom. I wish you would be always alright. God bless you!"

I was flooded with many wonderful memories of my father, but thoughts of his recent death were never far from my mind. These conflicting feelings became a source of inspiration for an ode to my father that I later wrote. I thought it would be both healing for me and respectful to my father to express my gratitude towards him through poetry.

ON THE LOSS OF MY FATHER

My humble dad!
Alas! I was not with you
When you breathed your last.
And it left a scar in my heart.
Never is there a remedy
To solace the pain caused by your loss.
Life without you is hard to bear
And words cannot express this grief.
Saddened that Death took you away,
But confident you've joined the saints,
And now live in the Garden of Eden
Happily ever after.
I'm grateful I had such a father,
The embodiment of genuine virtues:
Devotion, loyalty, and selflessness.
A man of honour and dignity,
Always a giver you were
Not expecting any to reciprocate.
All inspired by your caring heart,
Generosity, hospitality, and forbearance.
I still feel you with me
Each day of my life.
Memories of you enliven
Your image that lingers
And your legacy that stands
Forever in my mind.

My eyes were full of tears when I finished the poem.

When Abdul and Pedram found out about my dad's death, they came upstairs to my room to offer their condolences. At church, after the service, Grace gave a talk about my father, after which everyone hugged me and expressed how sorry they were for my loss.

CHAPTER 30

Level 2 Community Interpreting course started in September at Community Centre in Stockton-on-Tees. The course was intense and eighteen weeks long.

I had a wonderful teacher who knew her profession well and was greatly loved by all her students. Her name was Samantha. She showed great commitment to the course and had a true desire to improve our skills. Without exaggeration, she was one of the best teachers I had ever known. She understood the benefits of teamwork, the power of keeping things simple and practical, and the importance of good communication. These were just a few of the various techniques and methods she employed, and which we benefited, in addition to her kind, polite, and patient behaviour.

I loved learning from her, but I also liked my class because I had fabulous classmates from many different countries: Romania, Poland, Iraq, India, Tunisia, Palestine, and Belgium. Each of us different, with unique stories, but all of us with similar aspirations of rebuilding our lives in the UK.

There was another tutor who taught the same course at this college, and who was as capable and professional as Samantha. Her name was Amelia, and she was a stunningly beautiful. Her smile was radiant, and she was always dressed to kill, and sporting smart, blacked-framed glasses. She was, at the same time, serious about her work, her career and maintaining a consistent professional demeanour.

While studying the interpreting at this college, I started working for Language and Imperial, a company that supplied professional interpreters to public organisations such as GP practice.

CHAPTER 31

On 19th September 2018, I received a letter from Home Office. I could guess what the content was—The Determination of Asylum Claim –but I didn't have the guts to open it. Abdul was sitting by my side, praying the result would be positive. He started reading Al-Fatiha, the first Sureh of the Quran because he was a Muslim and I did the Lord's prayer, Our Father Who Art in Heaven.

I opened the letter while grasping for breath, to my amazement, I saw that I was granted asylum for five years. It was one of my best moments after my father's death. Abdul believed that God answered to our prayers. Then I began to cry tears of joy.

Abdul went to the kitchen and after a few seconds, he brought tea and chocolates.

"Let's celebrate your victory, Cyrus."

"Thank you, Abdul, thank you so much. I hope you'll receive a letter from Home Office very soon inviting you for interview."

"Pray for me, Cyrus."

"I do. You're in my prayers, Abdul."

After I left Abdul, I called Grace to inform her about the letter to make her happy because I was always in her prayers.

"Well done, Cyrus. Thank you for sharing this news. Let's celebrate your success. Rayan and I will be at 5 pm if it is ok with you. We'll pick you at the door. We'll go somewhere together."

Then I called Natalie who had recently started the Beta Course at Botolph church. Natalie started this course to help us develop our faith and personal lives. Previously, there was Alpha that was an evangelistic course. Its objective was to introduce the basics of the Christian faith through a series of talks and discussions. Beta is for those who finished Alpha and wanted to strengthen their understanding of what it really means to be a follower of Jesus.

Every four sessions Natalie took the Beta group somewhere outdoors, for pleasure. She once took us to a Bowling club in Middlesbrough. Next time we went for a walk in Stewart Park, but before the walk, she took us to a Fish and Chips on the house. Stewart Park was a public park, located in south Middlesbrough, next to the Captain Cook birthplace Museum. In this Park one can see a range of domesticated animals like rabbits and deer, llamas, and goats. Visitors can also see guinea pigs in the park.

We enjoyed the walk and, of course, the Fish and Chips.

Ryan and Grace arrived at 5:30 pm. They were very happy for the Home Office result. Ryan drove the white Toyota car towards the centre. Next to Middlesbrough library, there was a parking area, so Ryan stopped the car there. Then we walked towards Marks and Spencer which was in Linthorpe road. We went inside.

"We took you here to give you a gift on your success from Ryan and me."

"Wow! Look at that! I'm very surprised. I can't really say anything. Thank you so much. You made my day."

"That's ok, Cyrus. You can buy anything you like for £200.00"

I chose white shirt, slim blue jeans, and white underpants. Then we had coffee at Esquires Coffee, a short walk from Marks and Spencer.

Natalie invited me to a lunch at their house for Sunday after the church service. She lived with John, her husband, and her four children. What a lovely family!

On 20 September, I had a call from Armin, my old friend and colleague. I was delighted to hear from him since we had lost contact for about seven months. Luckily there was nothing risking his life and safety. After leaving his house, Armin was worried about my safety, so he tried to contact the smuggler. His mobile had been off all the time.

Then he wanted to call my family, but he refused because he thought he would risk their lives, being old and sick.

On Sunday, after the church service, Natalie and John took me to their home as they had previously arranged it. They had four children — two boys and two girls. The family all served Jesus Christ. In addition to her main profession as a teacher at primary school, Natali, a vocalist, singing soprano at church, was in charge of Beta course. Their children from top, Henry played guitar and would sing duet with his sister, Emma. Oliver was good at drum and Evelyn, still a student. John sometimes helped with the church services, although, he was very busy with his career, as a joiner.

We had chicken for lunch with mashed potato, boiled broccoli, and carrot. I had great time with the family, especially when Oliver took me to his room and played drum for me, accompanied with Henry's guitar. I left their home, and I promised next time I would make Iranian food for them.

CHAPTER 32

The following Monday, after Welcome Break, I had two interpreting assignments one at GP practice, and the other at Dental Clinic.

It is very exciting and encouraging to help clients with interpretation. The Community Interpreting course was very useful and practical because I learned that community interpreting is not just translating orally the words of a person speaking a different language. As an interpreter one should stick to and respect Ethical Principles or Code of Conduct. A community interpreter must consider the following tips when doing an assignment.

- Maintain confidentiality at all costs.
- Remain totally impartial.
- Interpret everything that is said faithfully and accurately—Transparency.
- If you think you made a mistake, go back, and correct it.
- Pursue ongoing education and training—new terminology, new idioms, and dialects.
- Manage the time.
- Avoid actions that discredit the interpreter's profession.
- Share professional knowledge with colleagues to improve your work.

I had to leave my house at Hope Street until the end of the month. It came in a letter from the organisation that said I should evacuate the property and rent an accommodation myself, but because I was out of work, I was allowed to apply for benefits including Housing Benefits. By taking the Community Interpreting Course, I hoped I could find a job after finishing the course and the training.

Grace helped me with a new accommodation as it was not easy to rent one. To rent an accommodation, a guarantor was needed and a full-time job. Grace knew a priest who had moved to another city and his house was empty, so she became my guarantor, and I rented the house.

It was a large three-bedroom house, located near Botolph church, in Albert Road. It was a temporary accommodation because I had something in mind—maybe to move to London after I finished my course.

I stayed in the new house for six months. I could not find a permanent job, having only two or three interpreting assignments a week was not enough and difficult to make ends meet.

My friends from Botolph church were unhappy about my decision to leave Middlesbrough, but they agreed with me that my future and my profession were of top priority. Some friends did their best to find a job in Middlesbrough for me to help me stay in the city, but it didn't work.

I myself didn't like the idea of leaving Middlesbrough. It was not easy to disconnect myself from the lovely people I met, nor the church I had come to consider my spiritual home as my home. My hopes and aspirations flourished here. Everything I had was due to church members who had accepted me as part of their family.

I invited Abdul to lunch with me in my home because I wanted to see him again before leaving Middlesbrough.

"Thank you for inviting me, Cyrus."

"You are welcome. We haven't seen each other since I left Hope Street."

"Why are going to leave Middlesbrough?"

"I couldn't find a full-time job here. I want to try my luck in London."

"I'm sure you'll make it there because in the capital there are a huge variety of jobs. There are also many places and attractions that you can visit and enjoy in London when you are free. It is not like Middlesbrough, where shops close in the early evening and the town becomes dark and quiet."

"I hope so. By the way, yesterday, I composed a poem for you to show my gratitude for supporting me during my stay in your house."

As Abdul was from Afghanistan, I chose Afghanistan as the title of the poem since I wanted to dedicate it to all the people of Afghanistan who were suffering under the Islamist rule of the Taliban.

AFGANISTAN

Freedom lost once more.
Was just touching sublime
Suddenly, he witnessed an abrupt reverse—a "Wasteland" now.
Women forced to abandon
Their aspirations and dreams.
How frightening it will be
Life without desire or ambition.
Evil wants to take our identity away from us.
Steal our individuality.
I remember Afganistan
Obtained it not with ease.
Suffered for decades,
Sacrificed, and
Lost so much.
Now strive to grasp it again.
Must stand on his own feet
As he had done it before.
Afghanistan needs another upheaval,
a voice is calling:
They deserve a beautiful life.
They deserve to live the way they want.
They deserve to be free, independent, and safe.

When I finished the poem, I saw that tears were streaming down his face.

"Thank you, Cyrus, thank you. It was the best gift I have ever received from anyone."

"I hope you'll get British citizenship very soon and see your family here."

CHAPTER 33

I n early February 2019, I moved to London. I rented a small studio flat through an agency online. It was situated in the City of Westminster, a borough which forms part of central London. Although the room was very small, it seemed like a big start toward a better future ahead of me because it was while living there that my partner came to join me in the UK.

After I received my BRP or Biometric Residence Permit card in Middlesbrough, in September 2018, I found out by a friend who was also an interpreter that a refugee who had Refugee Status could bring his or her spouse or partner which was known as 'refugee family reunion.'

He advised me to get help from British Red Cross located in Stockton-on-Tees. One day I went there to see if I could bring Raha, my partner, from Iran.

I had been in partnership with Raha for five years. We were in touch for quite a while after I left Iran. I intended to travel to Turkey to get married with her in order to facilitate her coming, but a biometric card was a prerequisite to any administrative or office activities. For example, if I wanted to open an account, or get a Driver's Licence, the BRP would be requested.

I didn't believe I could ever make it until I met Mary Renders. She would come to the British Red Cross once a month to give free advice to refugees and asylum seekers.

Mary Renders encouraged me to pursue the claim. I learned that through both marriage and partnership, partners could claim it as a Family Reunion.

At first, I took it for granted. I called Raha to tell her what the lawyer had said to me.

"We will never see each other again," she said while tears were streaming down her face. "It's difficult to believe what you are saying," she added.

"Let's have a go at it. It's worth trying."

Raha was a colleague of mine from the primary school. I saw her for the first time during a break while she was having her lunch.

Raha was of medium height. She was in her late thirties but looked younger than her age. She was slim and had long, thick, light brown hair and brown eyes. She was interested in her schoolwork, dedicating her time to her students—a committed teacher. She was loved by her students.

When I met her, she was eating Khoresh Gheimeh in the Teacher's Room.

Khoresh Geimeh is a very traditional and popular Iranian stew which is made from beef or preferably lamb, and split peas. It is served with rice. Other ingredients include fried onion, fried thinly-sliced potato, Limoo Amani or dried lemon and tomato paste.

Raha shared her lunch with me, putting half of the rice on a plate with the stew on top. I didn't say no because I was very hungry, and the food looked so delicious. I couldn't help myself. It made my mouth water.

Our first rendezvous was in Darband, which in Farsi means 'the door of the mountain.' It was the beginning of a hiking trail into Mount Tochal. Darband was a good place to visit and experience a little nature close to Tajrish, Tehran. There was a ravine with water flowing through it with restaurants and cafes surrounding the water.

"How can we proceed?" she asked.

"Mrs Renders advised me to collect documents, letters and photos to start with."

"What letters and photos?"

"Letters written by family members, relatives, and friends that certify or prove you and I have been in relationship. We should also

95

gather any photos we have taken in WhatsApp and telegram as a proof of our partnership."

I liked the communal kitchen of the new studio flat. It was a sort of favourite hangout for the residents of the building. In the kitchen I met people from different countries — Japanese, Italian, Russian, American, and Chinese. We had fabulous conversations with each other in that kitchen while eating our meals. We talked about food, our work, and the countries where we came from. We had in common the sad feeling of missing our country, our home, our family, and our friends.

I found a church near my flat, so I decided to go there on a Sunday in July 2019.

The flat had easy access to bus stops and a tube station. The very famous Oxford Street was only about twenty minutes' walk from my flat. Some of the very best shops and brands were found on this street such as Selfridge's, John Lewis, House of Fraser, M&S, Primark, and Gap among others.

Oxford Street was one of the busiest shopping streets in London, always lively and crowded. It was also a popular place for protests and demonstrations, with crowds starting from marble Arch or nearby Speakers' Corner.

Raha called me to check a few documents and letters with me. I was supposed to send them to my adviser in Middlesbrough. Fortunately, we had so many photos with Raha in WhatsApp and telegram.

On Friday, July 2019, I received a card from Grace and Ryan. They had been in Cyprus for two weeks. I was amazed that they were still remembering me after I left them.

CHAPTER 34

One Sunday around 10:30 am I left the flat to go to church. It was not too far away.

It was a warm sunny day—so beautiful! The streets were rather empty, but I could still see red single and double-decker buses passing by.

I entered St John's church. Most of the pews were full, but people were still coming in. Some went upstairs to the second-floor gallery. I was seated in the last row of pews in the back. As I was looking around, I heard someone speaking Farsi, my language, on his mobile. After the service, I approached him to introduce myself.

"Hello sir. I overheard you were talking Farsi. I see you are from Iran. How are you? I'm Cyrus." Then we switched to our mother tongue.

"Hi Cyrus. Nice to meet you. I'm Elvis."

"Nice to meet you too."

"What brings you here, to this church? Do you live in this neighbourhood?"

"Absolutely. I just moved to Westminster."

"Perfect Cyrus. I'm so delighted to see a fellow countryman here at this church."

Elvis was a short, stout man in his early sixties. He had a full beard and moustache and had a stern look about him, but I quickly learned he had a heart of gold.

"Let me introduce you to one of my best friends before we leave the church. I'm sure you'll like him," he said. He had a wide smile on his face.

"Sure. I would like that," I said.

"There he is! David, this is Cyrus, from Iran."

"Nice to meet you, Cyrus," David said. He seemed warm and friendly. "Khoobi? which in Farsi means, are you fine? He then smiled. "I'm interested in Farsi. I had an Iranian friend in the US. I know some Iranian foods. For example, Okra stew is khoshmazeh!"

"Happy you like Iranian food and our language, David." I returned his smile. "I'll invite you for an Iranian meal someday, as soon as I settled down."

David was a tall, good-looking guy in his mid-sixties. He was an American who had recently come to London working for an insurance company. He looked smart in his neat clothes and tidy appearance. He was nice to everyone in the way he talked and treated people at the church. To sum up his character, he seemed he was a gentleman from sole to soul.

David was happy that Elvis made friends with me at the church.

"I'd like to invite you to lunch in a restaurant to celebrate our new friendship with Cyrus," he said to me and Elvis. "I'll let you know about the address and date," David said and then departed.

Elvis and I left the church and took a walk towards the Baker Street tube station.

"Let's go to a bar and have a drink. There's one near here, if you have time."

"Yes, sure. I'm game."

We entered the City Bar and found an empty table.

"What would you like to drink?" he asked.

"I think I'll have beer," I said.

"Would you like to try a shandy? It is beer mixed with lemon, which makes it a bit lighter and tastier."

"Ok, sure. Thanks."

Elvis returned with JD and coke for himself and a pint of shandy for me.

"When did you come to the UK?" I asked.

"Around thirty years ago. First my mother came, then she invited me."

"What about you? How long have you been here?"

"Since March 2018."

"With your wife."

"No, I'm single, but I have a partner in Iran. She lives in Tehran. I talked with a solicitor to see if she can help me with bringing her over."

"I hope so. It's good to have someone with you. It's hard to live alone," he said. "What was your profession in Iran?"

"I was a teacher," I said. "David seems like a nice guy. I enjoyed his company. He was great fun."

"I see him every week. I have known him for two years. He usually comes with his friend, Albert. Both are perfect gentlemen, polite, and well-mannered. They treat the other church members with respect."

We left the bar and walked down Baker Street towards Marble Arch. We stopped to take a few pictures, then continued walking until we reached the Italian Gardens in Hyde Park. From there we strolled along the Long Water and Serpentine Lakes until we stopped at a spot between the Italian Gardens and the Arch by Henry Moore. Elvis took some monkey nuts out of his bag.

"Let's enjoy our time feeding birds and squirrels," he said.

We waited for a short time, holding the peanuts out in our hands, to tempt the squirrels and birds into grabbing them. In an instant, parrots began to sit on his shoulders and hands eating the peanuts. It was one of the nicest and most beautiful scenes I had ever seen. Then we took a walk towards Serpentine Lake and saw a display of different birds in the air, in the water and on the bank. There was a large variety of birds, large and small, with funny names such as Bewick's Swans, Whooper Swans, White-fronted Geese, Wigeons, Garganeys, Long-tailed Ducks, Scaups, and Scoters. Elvis gave me some bread he had in his bag and told me to feed the birds as well. I liked it because when I started feeding the birds, their numbers increased. In a flash we were surrounded by them. The joy I was granted by these beautiful creatures was tremendous.

I was on the way back home on a single-decker when I received a message from David suggesting we meet for lunch at Casablanca Restaurant on Marylebone Street, the following Sunday after church.

CHAPTER 35

I resumed my job as an interpreter in London, but, unfortunately, there weren't enough assignments for me to make ends meet. In comparison with Middlesbrough, the number of assignments in London was very low. So I decided to try another profession alongside the interpreting job.

I went to Jobcentre Plus to see if my work coach could help me with a course leading to a future job. I was advised to take an Events Steward course. Stewarding was a service that ensured the safety of spectators attending events such as indoor or outdoor festivals, sports tournaments, or concerts. I felt I had the stated skills for the course needed:

> Excellent communication
> Problem-solving abilities
> Highly responsible, and reliable
> Ability to work well under pressure.
> Ability to focus on guest needs
> Always Remaining calm and courteous

I really liked the course, which was held in a college in Wembley. It was a two-week intensive course —both exciting and useful.

Elvis called me on Saturday, the day before David's invitation for lunch. He wanted to know if I had time to accompany him to National Gallery in Trafalgar square. I accepted his invitation because I was fond of art.

I enjoyed my time at the gallery with Elvis, for I viewed the works of very famous painters, architects, and designers, including paintings from the likes of Picasso, Raphael, Manet, Gainsborough, Reynolds, Rembrandt, Rubens, Van Dyck, Gerard David, Rogier Van der Weyden, and so many others. It took us more than four hours to explore these masterpieces.

We left the gallery and walked towards Piccadilly Circus, a road junction and public space, and one of the city's top landmarks located in Westminster. It was famous for its neon signs and different displays, and it was a busy meeting place and tourist attraction.

On Saturday evening before I went to bed, I received a message from David, wanting to confirm lunch on Sunday.

On Sunday I got to St John's church at about 10:30 and saw Elvis and David sitting together in the middle on one pew. David introduced me to his friend Albert who was as tall and good-looking as David, and very sociable too.

We shook hands and then he gave me a friendly smile.

"We have two other guests joining us for lunch, Cyrus, Fr Simon and Fr Joshua," David said. Then "Let's get ready for the service. It's about to start."

Casablanca was a chic Swiss restaurant in the heart of Marylebone and near our church. I liked the charming atmosphere, and excellent service there, as well as the delicious food. I chose the chicken schnitzel and it arrived beautifully cooked and very delicious.

Each of us ordered something different, and the result was a great varied display of dishes: roasted Cod, Seared Trout, Grilled Sea Bass, and for me, Chicken Schnitzel. We enjoyed them all with a German Riesling that David had recommended, and it paired with our dishes marvellously.

"I hope your partner comes soon to join you, and we celebrate her coming together," said David as a toast with the wine.

Two months later in mid-September 2019, I received an email from my solicitor saying that Raha's visa case was complete and ready to be sent to VFS in Tehran with all the required documents, including my appointment letter.

I forwarded all of it to Raha to make copies, though She would have to take the originals. I still had doubts about her successfully being granted the visa, since we were not married. She had only one week for the appointment.

The stewarding course ended on 20 September 2019, and I was connected with an Events and Security company. My first work shift started, and I was sent to Millwall Football Club to work as a steward. It was very exciting to see the footballers and their supporters in person.

The match was between Millwall vs Charlton. I saw such excitement—even vehemence— in the spectators, especially in the parents with children who loudly supported their favourite team. They were full of passion and originality.

I had seen English teams play on TV when I was in Iran, but I never thought that I would someday watch them live on the pitch. I was delighted to be among the spectators, watching them shouting, applauding, and sometimes even swearing.

CHAPTER 36

I was very lucky that the approval for Raha's visa finally came. She couldn't believe it herself.

She flew to London on an Iranian flight on 8 October 2019. I was at Heathrow Airport for two hours waiting before her plane finally landed. Elvis was also with me. When he had found out that Raha was coming, he asked if he could come with me to the airport to greet her.

We bought a bouquet of flowers on the way to the airport, ready and eager to welcome her. It was 1:15 pm.

"Her plane lands in half an hour," Elvis said.

"She should come through around 2 pm," I said.

We waited somewhere close-by with our eyes glued to the Terminal 3 arrivals gate.

"There she is!" I suddenly exclaimed, running towards Raha with ecstasy. I hugged her tightly, holding the flowers with one hand and her waist with the other.

"Welcome to the UK, darling," I said, "I can't believe it, Rara." Then I gave her a kiss on her cheek and caught a whiff of her familiar perfume.

"Yes, it's true. I'm here," she said through tears of relief and joy.

"How was your flight?" I asked.

"It was fine," she replied.

Though she was still giddy with excitement, I could see a twinge of doubt or uncertainty in her face that was mixed with joy as if she couldn't fully believe that she was really, finally in the UK with me. She had suffered badly during our long separation. I was moved by her diminished look. I could see the suffering she had endured in her eyes, and on her face, but I was relieved to also see that She was relaxed now, and calm.

She was wearing a red shirt and black jeans. Her long, straight hair was dyed blond which had made her more attractive.

"Look at her!" Elvis said, grinning widely at her. "Welcome Raha."

"Oh sorry. Let me introduce my friend to you. This is Elvis, the only Iranian who comes to our church."

"Happy to meet you, Elvis."

"I am also very pleased to meet you, Raha," he said. "And happy to see you both smiling now."

"Thank you so much Elvis," Raha and I said together.

"I'd like to invite you to lunch in a restaurant and celebrate you and Raha's reunion. There is a nice restaurant in Marylebone. So let's take the Piccadilly line tube to Baker Street Station."

Elvis helped me with Raha's luggage. We took the Piccadilly line and changed at Green Park, taking the Jubilee line to Baker Street Station. We left the station and walked for about 10 minutes until we got to Silver Deer Restaurant. The menus came.

"Ok. What would you like to have, Raha?" I said. "Let me help you. I recommend you try the Fish and Chips, as it is a popular English meal."

"Yes, Cyrus is absolutely correct. Fish and Chips is pure English, and very popular in the UK. The meal consists of fried battered fish, usually haddock or cod, served with Chips."

"Ok I try it. Thanks," she said with a smile.

"Wow! You're making my mouth water. Hurry up please!" she smiled then we all burst into laughing.

David sent me a text message as we were eating. He wanted to know if Raha had safely arrived. His response to the news made him very happy.

"Ok, we'll see you in church this Sunday. Congratulations, Cyrus."

We toasted Raha's coming to the UK with champagne. Then started the lunch.

"I like the fish and chips. It's so delicious!"

We left the restaurant. We walked together to Baker Street Station, where we went our separate ways.

The flat was too small for the two of us, but we had to wait until the tenancy agreement came to an end. Raha was quite surprised at the size of the flat.

"There is not enough room to swing a cat," she said with a smile.

"Yes, too small. Now that you are here, we should move to another property."

"It doesn't matter now. I am just happy to be with you," she said.

Two days later, on 10 October, I had a shift scheduled at work. The match was between Millwall and Wigan Athletic. Raha was delighted that I had a job, but the Stewarding job was like Interpreting because there wasn't enough work for me to make ends meet in an expensive city like London. I was forced to stay on Universal Credit until I could sort out a permanent job for myself.

On the way back home, I called Raha and asked her to get ready to go out.

"We both need a change. Let's go out and paint the town red, as they say here. Let's do something to forget all the suffering we have faced."

"Where to?"

"Would you like beer?"

"Yes. Sure."

"There is a nice English bar on George Street. It's called 'Angel on Horseback.'"

It was a lovely old bar in the heart of Marylebone, and I had been there a few times. It was one of my favourites in London. Once inside there was a relaxed and warm atmosphere with friendly and welcoming staff. One day, before Raha's arrival to the UK, I was very sad and had asked Elvis to come with me to the bar. We sat outside at a wooden table. I liked the place since I could watch all the passers-by while drinking beer.

Raha and I went to the Globe Theatre to watch a performance of Hamlet, Shakespeare's longest play. I had bought the tickets online the night before. I knew she was interested in Shakespeare's works.

The Globe Theatre or Shakespeare's Globe was an Elizabethan playhouse for which Shakespeare wrote his plays. It was located in the borough of Southwark in London, on the banks of the River Thames.

We both were stunned by the place, the professional actors on the stage, the eager spectators, and the cosy atmosphere. I liked the simplicity and elegance there, as well as the great theatre history it represented.

I had seen Hamlet in Farsi in Iran and that had been perfect, but this production was quite original and unique. We loved it.

After the play, we walked along the River Thames towards London Bridge and from there to Tower Bridge. We were very impressed by the size of Tower Bridge. Tower Bridge took its name from the Tower of London, which was next to it, and which could be seen from afar. Although it was raining and windy in the evening, it was worth visiting. The lights at night made the bridge illuminous. It was a great experience for us because from atop the bridge we could see many famous London sights such as the Tower of London, London Bridge, the Shard, the HMS Belfast, Britain's Royal Navy, which was used during WWII, the Timepiece Sundial, Horsley down Steps, the Girl with Dolphin, and Butlers Wharf.

As we were tired, I thought it better to go back home and resume the tour for another day.

At 8 pm, that same day, my mother called me. She was very happy that Raha was in London with me. "I'm so happy to see you with Cyrus. I was concerned that he is all alone, and it was especially worrying after his father's death. Thank you, Raha, for being part of his life."

"It's very kind of you. I hope I can someday pay Cyrus back for his kindness and all his efforts for bringing me to the UK."

"God bless you."

"Thank you, mom. How're you doing?"

"I'm fine. Thanks. Today I went to the cemetery to see your father. I have missed him these days."

"He's always in my thoughts and prayers, mom."

CHAPTER 37

A Friday morning in November, Raha and I went to St Pancras Church in London not far from our flat. There were free English classes held in the church where Fr Simon had advised Raha to go. We liked the amazing atmosphere and the friendly and warm staff who worked there. I thought it was a suitable place for Raha to learn English, and to get acquainted with English society. Raha's class started at 2 pm on Monday. It was her first session.

Oxford Circus was near the church, so I hung around and window shopped to pass the time while Raha was in her English class at St Pancras Church.

Raha called me afterwards to fetch her. When I saw her, she was over the moon about the English class.

"How was the class today?"

"I really enjoyed my class. I was impressed with the quality of the material as well as the level of our teacher. The atmosphere was incredible. It is more than just an English language class. I can meet people from other parts of the world and we all can share our learning experiences with each other. I loved seeing the people there sitting and chatting with each other over tea and coffee. They are all so welcoming and friendly."

"Yes, it is really great for individuals who are looking for community in London, especially if they are new to the city."

"What is your teacher's name?

"Sarah, I guess, is her name."

"When is your next session?"

"The class is held twice a week—Mondays and Wednesdays."

December was approaching and people were preparing themselves for Christmas and New Year's. December was the most magical month in London with festivities, illuminations, the shimmering stars, and crowds of shoppers from around the world. The red double-decker buses, which would come and go endlessly, made London a very lively city. Oxford and Regent Streets were usually the first in London to switch on their Christmas decorations.

David invited us to lunch at his home two weeks before Christmas.

"Albert and I are going to the US for Christmas and New Year's. So we decided to see you beforehand and celebrate Raha's arrival," David said. "I'd like to cook one of my favourite dishes for you. It is a dish made with Okra, and I think you Iranians might like it."

"Oh really? We like okra so much. What do you call it?"

"Shrimp Okra Gumbo. But before I can prepare it, I need to know if you both can eat pork and shrimp."

"Yes. That is kind to ask, but we both sometimes eat ham. Though, we've never had it in stew! We would love to try it."

"Great. We can't wait to see you and Raha next week, then."

"Thank you so much for the invitation."

As David was very kind to us, Raha and I thought it would be a good idea to take something especial as a host gift.

"Let's buy Termeh, a type of Persian handwoven cloth, from an Iranian shop. We are sure he would like it. He can use it as a tablecloth. We can also buy some Iranian sweets such as Gaz, Persian Nougat, and Kolompeh, Iranian pastry."

"Yes, it is the least we can do to show our gratitude for his kindness and generosity."

On Wednesday Raha went to St Pancras Church for her English class. She showed much interest in her class sessions and did her homework with enthusiasm. It was a good way for her to socialise and mix with people, and I was very happy that she was doing so well. Raha knew a little English, but it was not enough to handle a conversation. she needed to get more acquainted with the various English accents, including proper intonation as well as the slang and idiomatic expressions used by native speakers. English is much more than knowing words and grammar. Language is part of a culture, and as culture can influence the way a person thinks or behaves, language also can shape thought and behaviour. People express their feelings and emotions through language. Language is not just a tool for communication, but an essential factor in acceptable social behaviour. Acceptable behaviour is learned by observing and imitating the behaviour of others. It is something to do with psychology—environment affects our behaviour so individuals can learn behaviour through observation. A non-native speaker should learn behaviour the way children do, by imitating family members, friends, famous figures, and even fictional television characters. If they are rewarded for getting behaviour right, they in turn reinforce the behaviour for others.

Raha came back home by herself using google map, as I had taught her. It was one of the things she needed to learn, how to navigate the city.

Raha was delighted that her teacher, Sarah, had given her personal contact number to help her with English. Raha later called on Sarah several times to resolve a few grammatical questions and Sarah was so kind and helpful, replying to Raha with great eagerness.

On the second Sunday of December, at 12:30, we went to David's apartment. Albert was also there helping David with the lunch. They both welcomed us warmly. We liked his flat, as it was luxuriously furnished. We were amazed by the many lovely things he had used to decorate his flat, and by the friendly feel of his place. We were also happy that Albert had been invited.

David liked our gifts, especially the Termeh. We had a small gift for Albert too. Wine quickly came and David made a toast to Raha and her arrival in London.

The Shrimp Okra Gumbo was delicious. It was like a stew with a nice blend of Okra, Shrimp, and smoked pork sausage. It was quite different from the Okra stews we knew, but it was very appetising. David made a truly memorable day for us.

On Christmas Eve, we went to church. Elvis was also there, sitting in the last row, and we sat next to him. Christmas Eve, or the night before Christmas Day, was a festive tradition to commemorate the birth of Jesus. It was one of the most significant celebrations in the Christian world. There was usually a Midnight Mass on Christmas Eve which was a popular festive custom. The Mass included the celebration of Holy Communion. The service consisted of hymns about Christmas, Christmas Carols, and readings from the gospels telling the Christmas story. The entire church was lit with the glow of candles.

It was my second time - but Raha's first- to experience Christmas. She was delighted by the festive decorations, lights, and carols. We missed David and Albert, but happy that Elvis was with us. Fr Simon and Fr Joshua were imposing figures with their white and gold robes. The service went on for around two hours. We also had wine and cookies afterward, under the church's portico.

We moved to a new flat in Cricklewood in mid-March 2020. The new place had more space and was suitable for two of us. The flat was furnished, on the ground floor, and had one bedroom, a living room, and a tiny kitchen.

When Sarah found out that we were going to move, she asked Raha if we needed her help in moving our stuff with her own red Toyota car.

Our move coincided with the outbreak of Covid-19 pandemic. A national lockdown with severe restrictions were introduced in response to the number of deaths caused by the coronavirus. The virus was first identified in Wuhan, China, in December 2019. Attempts to stop it failed, and the virus quickly spread globally. A pandemic was declared in March 2020 and from that point until July 2022, millions of lives were affected and lost. It was one of the deadliest disease outbreaks in history. A variety of vaccines such as Pfizer and AstraZeneca, were eventually produced and distributed worldwide. Those vaccines were very successful, especially alongside effective public health measures such as social distancing, high personal hygiene standards – masking, hand washing, and cleaning surfaces. The roll of governments and the role of each individual were both of great importance.

Raha and I were infected by Covid-19 on 11 January 2021. The NHS messaged us to stay at home, and we were sick enough to be bedbound for 11 days. Raha eventually recovered, but my condition grew steadily worse, and on 24 January, after Raha had encouraged me to get out of bed, as I had been asleep the whole day, I simply collapsed onto the floor. Raha was alarmed and frightened to see this and called 999 and soon afterward an ambulance arrived. My oxygen level had dropped to fifty, so I was taken directly to the Royal Free Hospital. I was in the hospital for nine days until I recovered thanks to the persistent efforts of medical staff. My wife's support and care for me was also of significance. I left hospital on the first of February. I continued to have breathing problems for another three months, during which I had regular chest scans and blood tests until I fully recovered. It felt like I was given a new lease on life after my recovery.

During my stay in the hospital, two of my favourite former Iranian national team footballers, Mehrdad Minavand and Ali Ansarian, tragically died from Covid-19 during a week of each other. I also lost my uncle, and a dozen other relatives.

During this time, we couldn't see any of our friends. We were not allowed to meet each other.

My mother was infected, but she recovered after two weeks. Elvis was also infected, recovered. Later on, David and Albert also tested positive.

CHAPTER 38

When I was in hospital, Ramtin, an old friend of mine, who lived in Barcelona, Spain, called me to see how I was. After the war between Iran and Iraq broke out, Ramtin's parents were in fear of losing their son in the war, so they sent him to Germany to build a new life there. He then was granted citizenship after a couple of years. In Germany he went to university and studied medicine, becoming a doctor, a urologist. Later, he left Germany for Spain and chose Barcelona as the city of his dreams. He had been living there for around two decades.

Ramtin was tall, and handsome. He was a pleasant, sociable guy in his early fifties. He was very neat and well-dressed. I remember the time when we were school friends; he was very smart and always received the highest grades. He spoke English fluently, although he had never left the country. When he talked to our teacher in English, my classmates and I were flabbergasted. He seemed to have an innate talent for every subject. He had a finger in every pie. Ramtin was not only good at schoolwork, but also in other areas such as in music and singing. I remember when he was still in Iran, we would meet in his parents' house and sometimes he would come to my home.

We had guitars and used to play and sing together. We would usually sing Beatles' songs such as 'Let It Be,' or 'Hey Jude', or from Elvis and Bee Gees. Sometimes we practiced in the bathroom because it echoed in there and our music seemed to become more beautiful. I went to a music academy to learn the guitar, but Ramtin learned it just by listening. He was so much better at it than I was. Ramtin always stood head and shoulder above everyone in everything. He was good at singing, at language, music, schoolwork, and anything else one could imagine.

In Iran, when we were school students, we were not allowed to play or even carry our musical instruments outdoors because they were forbidden. Chess and cards were also forbidden, as were many other things.

One afternoon Ramtin and I and two of Ramtin's friends went to Chaloos Road, one of the most beautiful roads in the world, with popular tourist attractions, tunnels, cafes, and restaurants. We stopped at a café and had tea next to the Karaj River and enjoyed our time. On the way back home, I started to play guitar and Ramtin and the other two accompanied me by singing 'Chera Nemiraghsi,' which in English means 'Why Don't You Dance.' It was dark, so Ramtin couldn't see the road well. The car fell into a huge hole on its side, by the road. Suddenly the nearby lights went off because the electrical wires were cut by the wheels. We left the car with difficulty, lucky that no one was injured. We couldn't get the car out of the hole, however. It was trapped. We were there until 2 am trying to find a lorry driver to help us get the car out of the hole, but none appeared. The place was around three miles far away from Karaj. In Karaj we found a large lorry parked in a street by a house. We knocked at the door and asked the driver to help us with the problem. He demanded a lot of money, but we were forced to accept it, sharing the expense between us. The reasons for such trouble were due to all the restrictions and interdictions we all faced in Iran. If we had been free, we wouldn't have had such a disaster.

Ramtin is now a practicing urologist in Barcelona, and he is also part of a choir, where his baritone voice has sung such classics as 'An den Mond, D193' by Franz Schubert. To sum up his character, he is perfect in what he does, a child prodigy turned renaissance man. He lives with his friend, Rafael, in a luxurious villa, set in a very beautiful, green area, in the upper part of the city, one of the most vibrant of Barcelona's neighbourhoods. Rafael is a chemistry teacher, good-looking and warm, in his fifties. They invited me to Barcelona several times, but due to some personal problems I haven't yet been able to make it there.

When I was sick with covid-19 during lockdown, Sarah and her husband, John, called us to say they were going to bring some provisions for us. They knew we couldn't go out because we both were isolating with Covid. They came into our parking area and dropped off two M&S plastic bags outside our door, while we waited inside wearing masks. We were all careful not to break the restriction rules.

When Raha opened the door to fetch the bags, she exclaimed "Look what they have brought!"

There were aubergines, tomatoes, carrots, onions, oranges, apples, grapes, pears, dates, a bouquet of flowers, and even a walnut cake that John had made. I called Sarah to thank her for what they had done. They were truly generous and good-hearted. What a sweet couple!

We were once invited for a coffee outdoors in Golders Hill Park, on 26 June 2021. It was a warm sunny day, very beautiful. Dozens of people were sitting at their tables, chatting and enjoying their time with friends or family members. To limit the spread of Covid-19, people kept a distance of at least one metre from each other.

"How's everything with you guys?" John asked.

"We are fine thanks."

"Would you like to travel to Scotland?" Sarah asked. "We have a cottage in Eyemouth. If you are interested, we would like to offer it you both for a week away."

"You'll enjoy your time there," John said.

"Why not! With pleasure. When can we go there?" Raha was overjoyed by this kind offer.

"We'll let you know about the exact time and date."

"I appreciate your kindness," I said.

"We'll give you maps and all the information you will need about the cottage and Eyemouth before your travel," Sarah said.

John and Sarah are amazing. Both are tall and in good shape, kind and helpful. John has PHD in chemistry and is in his early seventies and Sarah was a teacher and is in her mid-sixties. Raha and I have enjoyed their company and friendship, as well as their job advice.

In June 2021, we travelled to Eyemouth, Scotland, by train. The train had three stops, in York, Darlington, Newcastle and lastly, Berwick-upon-Tweed. It took about three hours and thirty minutes to get there. Then we took a bus to the cottage located in a suburb near the North Sea.

"Wow! What an enchanting town!" I said, admiringly.

"Yes. It is so beautiful!" Raha said.

Eyemouth was a small town in Berwickshire. It stood on the North Sea coast of the Scottish Borders, north of Berwick-upon-Tweed. Eyemouth had plenty to do, so it was a great place for tourists to spend the day. There was the North Sea. There was an imposing marine landscape, everywhere green, a beautiful harbour, the Fish and Chips restaurants, the fabulous path from Eyemouth to St Abbs, the dramatic cliff views, and the stunning lighthouse. Eyemouth and St Abbs were two of the most impressive and breath-taking places for anyone who was fond of beautiful coastal walking.

One day we went to The Lighthouse to have Fish and Chips. I had never ever seen such a nice place before. The meal was absolutely amazing. The staff was very friendly, and the location was stunning. It was situated just close to the Fisherman's Wharf, full of boats and ships.

On our second day we went to the wharf. We saw three guys unloading fish, shrimps, and lobsters. I asked one of them, a middle-aged, Scottish man, about the price of a fish which was very odd to us, broad-bodied and flat. I had never seen a fish like it.

"This is turbot Sir," he said with a wide smile. I liked his Scottish accent, although it was difficult for me and Raha to understand. Still, we found it very sweet.

"How much is it Sir?" I asked, returning his smile.

"Five pounds each," he said.

"Is it delicious?" Raha asked.

"Absolutely ma'am," he replied. "Turbot is the most expensive fish on the market and a highly valued food fish. Easy to cook ma'am."

"So, I want two please."

"Do you want me to clean them for you?"

"Yes please. Thank you so much."

He went inside the ship with the turbots. After five minutes, he came back with the cleaned fish.

"How much should I pay Sir?"

"No charge. You are my guests. Enjoy your meal." Then he explained how to cook it.

The large two-story cottage was close to Eyemouth, fully furnished, neat and tidy. There was a fireplace which warmed the house, and a beautiful patio was furnished with sofas and a table.

CHAPTER 39

When we returned to London, we saw Elvis only once. It was in July 2020. After the church service, as usual, we went to the City Bar, our favourite hangout. Elvis and I had JD with coke, and Raha chose a gin and tonic. We had a great time together, but sadly it turned out to be the last time we ever saw him.

In November, I sent Elvis a text but received no reply. In December, I sent him a Merry Christmas message, but still, no reply. Raha and I became very concerned about him and his health.

"Why hasn't he answered our calls?" I wondered.

"Maybe he is sick or in hospital." Raha suggested, looking worried.

"If he is in hospital, why should he turn off his mobile? Do you think he might have changed his number?" I asked Raha. I felt anxious and nervous. I had a bad feeling that something was very wrong, that he was sick or that he had died. The thought that he might have died was eating at me. I couldn't help thinking the other way. *Yes, he must be dead*, I thought. Although I was quite sure there was something wrong with him, I still hoped my guess was wrong.

We decided to go to Speakers' Corner, his hangout, hoping we might see him around. I called Fr Simon and Fr Joshua to see if they had any news about Elvis.

"I have no idea where he is. He hasn't appeared here since Christmas," Fr Simon said.

Fr Joshua said the same thing.

I remembered that in early 2020, Elvis suggested that we accompany him to a church near Bayswater Road. It was an Anglican church, beautiful with excellent music, good sermons, and liturgy. Elvis had wanted us to see a different church.

So, we planned to go there to see if the clergymen or even some churchgoers might know something about Elvis or his whereabouts.

We talked with a church priest. His tone changed as soon as I uttered Elvis's name. After a short pause, the priest told me that Elvis had died of heart attack in September 2021, but he was not sure if Elvis had died in hospital or in his bed at home. When we heard the news of Elvis's death, Raha and I had a suddenly chill, and we were unable to move, as tears streamed down my face and Raha started weeping. We couldn't imagine Elvis had left us.

How terribly sad!, we thought. All the time we were looking for Elvis, he had been dead all along!

"It's unbelievable!" How tragic!" I said.

"Where is he buried?" Raha asked.

"I have no idea, but I'll ask for you," the priest said. "I'm sorry your friend has passed away."

"Please let us know where he is buried," Raha said. Her eyes were still full of tears.

Elvis was single and lived in his own flat. His mother was the only person in his life. She was sick and very old. I was sure now that her son was dead, and she would be in a terrible state.

Raha and I couldn't sleep that first night after learning of Elvis's death. We couldn't stop thinking about him, wondering what we could have done, or should have done. It was bothering me. Why hadn't we seen him more before his death? But because of Covid-19 and the restrictions, we really couldn't see anyone during the pandemic, not just Elvis.

Raha reassured me that it had all been a simple and unfortunate misunderstanding. My guilt could not be assuaged. I got out of bed, as I was unable to sleep, and I made a coffee for myself. I picked up a piece of paper and a pencil and started to write a poem. I just wanted to write something to calm myself down. The result was the following poem.

HIS NAME WAS ELVIS
(Tribute On the Loss of a Lovely Friend)

Though so biased for his Christianity,
A bit tough in defending his beliefs,
Displayed 'Sound and Fury',
And sometimes 'Looked Back in Anger',
He proved a kind-hearted man and generous.
Was first to lend a hand, and willing.
On the first day we met at church in London,
Seated in the corner, calm and dignified.
After the service, approached to shake hands.
And he was first to break the ice.
To help us pass the time more agreeably,
Since we were alone and new here,
He invited us to McDonald's.
Took us to City Bar, cheers!
Gave us a tour of the city
Just to help us forget our troubles.

His name was Elvis.
Though an outgoing guy he was,
Socialised with anyone he met,
Lonely was he, so lonely.
Covid-19 lockdown closed all public gatherings.
People forced to stay at home.
And a distance grew between us.
So, we didn't see him, for a long while.
Unfortunately, 'has made all the difference.'

His name was Elvis.
Tried to get in touch, failed I.
Carried out a painstaking search, alas!
Decided I to seek help.
No one knew the reasons why he wasn't around.
No one cared what happened to him.

No one lifted a finger to look for him.
No one realised his absence
Despite his full presence.

His name was Elvis.
Elvis was short
But his character was big,
A man of great integrity.
Our friendship was brief,
But it felt I had known him for ages.

Yes, he was Elvis.
Died he in loneliness, finally.
Like anyone else,
Despite being among so many.

His name is Elvis.
You're never alone now son.
You have the Father with you
To take your hand.
You did your mission well.
There's no more suffering,
And no place for discomfort.

When I finished the poem, I read it to Raha. While reading, I saw tears trickling down her face.

The next day I had a call from the priest, and he told me that Elvis had been buried in Greenfield Cemetery. Poor Elvis!

On Sunday, after church, Raha and I decided to go to Greenfield Cemetery to find Elvis's grave. We bought Lilium and Chrysanthemum and then headed to the Cemetery.

We sat next to his grave, looking at his gravestone.

How odd! I was perplexed to see his surname for the first time. It was Parsa. Elvis Parsa, he was. I knew him only by his first name, just as others did. It didn't occur to me to ask him what his surname was, or where he lived. There were many questions I would have liked to ask him, to know more about him, but he was no longer here to reply. Something was eating me from inside. I felt a tingling sensation down my right side, all the way to my toes. It was very unusual.

It was a moment of truth, and recognition. I was experiencing something I had not noticed before. Why should I have postponed it? I should have contacted Elvis before he died.

The phrase 'It's never too late' does not work here. It is not applicable. We should all do something before it is too late. No one knows what is going to happen, or what tomorrow might bring. The phrase is used to encourage someone to try to accomplish something. It is true that you can always start something new any time you wish, no matter how long you have waited or how old you are. But for seeing your loved ones, it is not appropriate to wait. It may be, sad to say, too late if you wait. We cannot reverse this once done, so I disagree with this mindset. Life is extremely unpredictable. Time is passing very fast, and life is too short. So, it is better to be too early rather than too late.

Something was deeply upsetting me. I could have seen my parents at least once in another country, bordering Iran, like Turkey, but I didn't ever do that, unfortunately. I used to tell myself that there was still time. But what happened? I lost my father without having the chance to see him before his death.

There are people like me who think or feel like this, ignoring that 'Time's Winged Chariot' is always near. When it comes, nothing can get time back or stop it. What comes next? Suffering for what you have lost. You can do nothing to avoid it. Alas! We forget the sad lesson we have learned from our mistakes. Now I am feeling a change in me, after all that has happened during the pandemic and all the deaths of those dearest to us. I have come to realised that we must continue to live. Life does go on, but without those whom we love, it can seem meaningless and fruitless. So, we need to care about those we love since we are one body. There is a Persian proverb saying, 'if an organ or a limb gets hurt, the other organs or limbs cannot continue to exist.' All those who have come into my life, have had an important role on my spiritual growth.

CHAPTER 40

Months later, in April 2022, Mr Boris Johnson, the British Prime Minister, ended all Covid-19 pandemic restrictions and lockdown with a brief statement. Everything returned to normal. All public venues opened, such as cinemas, theatres, concerts, sports venues, and festivals along with restaurants and bars. It was all thanks to the persistent efforts of the government and the NHS medical teams for the hugely successful vaccination programme, and above all, the support and attention of the British people. Most of the people in the United Kingdom received at least three jabs of vaccines or boosters. We learned that we should learn to live with and manage the virus. Still, it could be everywhere. The 'Stay at home, protect the NHS, and save lives' campaign was launched by the government. It was the key message of the UK government to stop the spread of the Covid-19. The motto ran across TV, radio, and all other social media. Billions of pounds were spent to support a lockdown and to let the public stay at home. The British public made extraordinary sacrifices to help the government further its objectives.

Later, in 2021, Omicron, a new variant, broke out worldwide. It spread faster, but there was no evidence yet that it was causing a more severe illness than the previous variants.

This year, in 2022, Her Majesty the Queen became the first British Monarch in history to celebrate a Platinum Jubilee, marking the 70th anniversary of her accession to the throne. Celebratory events took place across the United Kingdom. It was an opportunity for the public throughout the UK to come together and celebrate the historic milestone.

During the ceremony, there was an opportunity to watch the events via large screens set up in St James' Park, as well as live on BBC, not just in the UK, but oversees too. Royal processions, Street parties, Big Jubilee Lunches, these were all part of the festivities.

At the Buckingham Palace, musicians and singers who performed included Sir Paul McCartney, Brian May (The Queen + Adam Lambert), Rod Stewart, Tom Jones, Annie Lennox, Ozzy Osbourne, Alicia Keys. An audience of around 12,000 people came together to the Palace's beautiful gardens. The Platinum Jubilee party was hosted by the Royal family and the BBC.

I talked with my solicitor to see if I could bring my mother to the UK for two or three months as a tourist. I had not seen her for about four years. The solicitor advised me to provide papers and documents to start the case.

I was not sure if I would ever see my mother here in the UK, but I didn't want to lose hope. I thought it was worth the time and the effort. I had to keep alive the hope I had to bring my mother here and reunite with her.

Lightning Source UK Ltd.
Milton Keynes UK
UKHW010644051022
409964UK00001B/141